tasty PICKLE

By JJ Knight

USA Today bestselling author of

Single Dad on Top
The Accidental Harem
Big Pickle
Hot Pickle
Spicy Pickle
Royal Pickle
Royal Rebel
Royal Escape
Tasty Pickle
The Wedding Confession
Second Chance Santa
Uncaged Love
Fight for Her
Reckless Attraction

Want to make sure you don't miss a release?
Sign up for emails or texts at www.jjknight.com/news

ABOUT THE TASTY EVERYTHING SERIES

★★★★★

K̦night is downright diabolical in her use of humor, starting us out with a my-drink-choked-me, hilarious opening scene, and it just gets funnier from there. ~ BookAddict

★★★★★

I'm passing out over here from that swoon. ~ Southern Chicks Lit

★★★★★

Tasty Mango causes belly aching laughing, with **full on tears running down your face from laughing so hard**. ~ Misty Reads Book Blog

★★★★★

This book had me laughing out loud too many times to count. Thelma of Thelma & Louise Book Blog

★★★ **TASTY PICKLE** ★★★

Surely nobody has ever met their great love while using duct tape to pull cactus needles out of their girl parts on a mountain trail.

Except I just did.

Let me tell you about Axel Pickle.

He's a bronzed god.

Totally outdoorsy.

Worth half a billion after selling his nature app.

And he hikes *naked*.

He showed up in nothing but his hiking boots when I ran shrieking onto his private property after peeing on a prickly pear and being unable to put my pants back on.

We've been staring at each other's private parts from the moment we first laid eyes on each other.

But I can't date him.

I shouldn't even talk to him.

And why he's showing up at the hotel deli where I work, volunteering to slice the salami is a mystery to me.

I'm running from a terrible situation, and I need to keep my head down and avoid the world.

But something about the way Axel looks at me gets under my skin.

And this time, no duct tape in the world can yank the hooks he's set in my wary, introverted soul.

Casey Shay Press
PO Box 160116
Austin, TX 78716
www.jjknight.com

Paperback ISBN: 9781938150982

1

———

AXEL

I'm pretty good at avoiding mosquito bites on my balls.

When your favorite pastime is hiking, and your preferred way of doing it is *naked*, you have to consider the possibility of bug attacks in tender places.

I have Mom to thank for the perfect solution. She never liked chemical sprays, so we avoided the industrial-grade insect repellent.

Her answer? Avon Skin So Soft. She slathered us in it as kids.

So, when I took up naked nature hiking, I never worried about having to hose down with something that might shrivel the family jewels. Just a quick swipe of Mom's all-purpose lotion, and I was good to go.

I took to streaking at an early age. Mom says she had to put sliding locks on the tops of the doors or else my squeaky-clean toddler self would slither out of her grasp after a bath and take off through the neighborhood, the wind in my baby-fine hair.

Sometimes, like today, when I'm picking my way over rock, I catch a whiff of that feeling from when I was little. The breeze on my body. The freedom of unconstrained movement. Nothing comes between me and the wide-open sky.

It's a Rocky Mountain high, and not the kind that's legal here in Colorado.

It's communion with nature.

The only complication besides bug bites was finding the right level of privacy.

Everybody carries a phone, and I don't need that kind of publicity.

So, I bought my own space.

The trails I hike are part of the acreage I purchased a couple of years back, after my life changed with the sale of a phone app I wrote. My parents also own a good amount of land nearby. Nobody should be anywhere near me, which makes the area safe enough for my hobby.

I hit a particularly tough stretch, a tall rock with scrub brush on either side. There's a decent length of trail leading to it, so rather than going for finger holds, I take off in a run, my hiking boots crunching the dirt, and leap up the side.

I roll at the top and quickly regain my footing. My gymnastics get me a scrape on my hip, but that's typical for a tough hike like this. Nothing worth wearing clothes for.

But once I'm back to walking, I'm surprised by a hint of human traffic. It's not much, just a suggestion of disturbed dirt, some bent branches, and a few small rocks kicked aside.

. It's enough to send me into the brush, though. I'd rather not surprise a stranger, even if they are on my land without permission. Out-of-town hikers in particular don't know when they're crossing unmarked property lines.

I keep winding my way up, aiming for a spot where I can look down and see if the visitors are still here, or if I've found old evidence.

I climb another slope and sit between two sections of brush to pull out my binoculars.

As I follow the walkable part of the mountainside, I see something. A bit of orange caught on a branch. I lean forward and twist the focus. It's a strip of nylon, the kind you tie on a tent stake so no one will trip on it.

Someone's camping nearby.

My urge is to get dressed. Somebody's been up here, and I don't want to encounter them as I am.

But my annoyance rises. I bought this land just for this feeling. The gritty rock against my skin. The sun warming my belly.

Besides, they might have been here weeks ago.

I peer at the sun, considering my position. I'm at the east-most stretch of my property. The next parcel over belongs to people I know. We're related in a roundabout way. My cousin Anthony married a woman named Magnolia Boudreaux, and her sister bought the land and built a wedding venue on it. A castle, in fact.

You can't see the castle from here. You'd have to go a lot higher to get the right vantage point. It's a good fifteen-mile hike with no established trailheads and several challenging cliff faces.

Still, I suppose it's possible someone might have set off from the castle, somebody skilled and prepared to camp.

I should probably get dressed.

I close my eyes and listen, really listen. It's early autumn, near-perfect hiking weather. A breeze coming off the mountain counteracts the sun bearing down. The leaves rustle as they dry out, preparing to fall. A few birds caw and whistle.

But no footsteps. No voices.

It's fine. That tent flag could be months old. Years, even.

I hop to my feet and survey the summit. I don't plan to reach it today. Getting somewhere isn't the point. It's all about the journey.

I'm ready to re-commune with nature, head west, and get away from the border of the two properties.

But then I hear it.

A shriek.

It's a woman.

Then steps.

Running steps.

Birds burst out of the trees about a hundred yards below.

Another scream, then an audible, "No, no, no, no!"

Definitely a woman.

And she sounds like she's in trouble.

I slide down the rock. When I hit flatter ground, I race in the direction of the disturbance. A few mountain critters scamper through the underbrush, away from whatever is crashing through the trees.

I spot flailing limbs and a hint of chestnut hair, then there she is.

A woman, petite, red-faced, and screaming.

And she's not wearing pants.

2

CALYPSO

I'm going to die on the side of a mountain with cactus spines in my hoo-haw, and squirrels will eat out my eyes!

I careen through the trees, hoping whatever vile creatures pelted me with nuts are long gone.

Then I crash into something solid, warm, and definitely human.

Oh, God, it's worse than killer rodents.

It's a man.

And he's… naked?

I let out another shriek and try to back away, but he has his arms around me.

"Let go! Let go!" I scream, my spit flying in his face.

He does, and I fall backward, sprawling.

This day could not get any worse.

First, I'm forced on a hike by my employer.

Then, I get tired and slow down for like fifteen seconds and somehow lose the group.

Then, I get pelted with nuts by maniac squirrels with a grudge.

I ran in the direction where I thought the group was headed and lost the trail completely. No one answered when I called out.

Of course, I had no cell signal.

Of course.

Just like a horror movie.

I headed back the way I arrived (I think) and started stress-drinking Gatorade.

Then, I had to pee.

So, I popped a squat.

Apparently on a cactus hidden in the brush.

Tiny spines attached to my girl parts.

I jumped away from it, and then I saw something flash by me. I was sure it was a mountain lion, or tiger, or bear. I don't know. I'm not Dorothy.

So, I ran for my life, yoga pants around my ankles.

I managed to get the pants off somewhere along the way.

And now, I'm here.

With a man.

A naked man.

I'm on my back, my cactus-impaled girl parts flashing in the sun, my yellow daisy underwear caught on my ankle.

Right now I would like very much to be eaten by a mountain lion.

I can think of nothing else to do, so I close my eyes, lay my head in the dirt, and wish for death.

Then something nudges my shoe.

Uggh.

I ignore it.

Nudge.

No. I'm dead. Death has become me.

Nudge.

"Hey."

He speaks.

I open one eye in a squint. He's standing over me like a bronzed god, naked as the day is long other than a backpack, a neckerchief, and hiking boots.

And I look.

Of course I look.

And whoa.

He's packing.

He must realize I'm looking because one eyebrow lifts. He opens his mouth like he might call me out on it, but then *he* looks.

Oh, right, I have a distinct lack of clothing from the waist down.

And I can't close my legs or I'll push the cactus needles farther in.

I close my eye again.

"We're a real pair," he says. I imagine that male member swinging back and forth. I shouldn't. But the sight of it is burned into my brain.

And I have to admit, I like his voice. It's low. Sexy. Rumbly. Maybe I'm already dead. He's the angel sent to carry me away.

Huh. I like this. I open my eyes again to see if he's real. Yep. Deep tan. God-like face. Pecs for days. Abs like an underwear ad. And, yeah. The best part. Damn.

"Are you okay?" He stares down at me, his gaze dropping to my naked bits, then flying up again.

Should you talk to an angel? What's the protocol here?

But I do. "Please tell me I'm dead."

That gets a smile. He tries to bite it back, since something serious could very well be happening. But damn, it's charming.

"You look very much alive to me," he says. "What happened?"

I want to cross my legs, but it's not possible. "I peed in the wrong place."

His need to drop his gaze again is palpable. His jaw ticks with the effort of not looking. "The wrong place?"

"Cactus."

His neck, previously as golden-tan as the rest of him, goes red. "So there's cactus needles in your…"

"Yes. And I'm being chased by maniac squirrels. And possibly a…" No. I'll stop there. That's enough.

"Did you poke yourself or…"

"No. Something's there. Something tiny and prickly stuck to me."

He lets out a long, slow breath. "Right. I know the variety. Do you need me to—"

"No! No. I can probably get them. I haven't had a chance." I can't meet his gaze.

He bites his lower lip, and it's ridiculously sexy. There's a rush to my parts, and owww. Yeah, no. Don't do that, body. Now is not the time to send any blood down there.

"Should I turn around?" he asks.

"Yeah. Probably."

He does, and dang, the back side is as nice as the front. Calves, thighs, butt. Zero tan lines Apparently clothes are not his thing.

I don't realize how long I've been sitting here staring until he says, "I've gotten the tiny clinging cactus spines before. They're called glochids."

I have to look. I sit up and bend over. This is the worst.

"How many are there?" he asks.

I peer down. "At least six. Maybe more. They're kind of small for how much they hurt. I didn't know they came out of the cactus."

"The big spines don't. But the small glochids are barbed, so they will easily attach to your skin if you brush against them. You didn't look first?"

I'd hoped to pee quickly and move away from the evidence. It might draw mountain lions, like sharks are drawn by blood. I don't know. I don't hike!

"I was in a hurry."

"Because of the maniac squirrels?"

I hate this. "Partly."

"Chickarees can get feisty if you get close to their tree nests."

"They threw nuts at me."

He chuckles. "I believe it."

He believes me. I'm not crazy. "Are there mountain lions?" I glance around as if saying their name might conjure one.

"That would be rare. They sleep through the day."

"Oh."

"How's it coming?"

I touch one of the spines, sucking in a breath at the pain. "They're too small to grab."

He nods. "I have some duct tape."

"Duct tape?"

"Yeah. The best way to get them out is to spread the tape over the area and then yank it off. The needles stick to the tape and come out."

That sounds like the world's worst Brazilian.

"You want me to get the tape?" His voice tells me he knows I'm concerned about trying this method.

"If you think it will work." I desperately want my panties back on. I have a pair of shorts in my backpack. I don't care about the yoga pants I lost.

He slides his backpack off his shoulders, and I'm treated to his entire backside. He clearly hikes a lot. His legs are tree trunks of muscle. His shoulders bulge.

I grimace at my pasty white legs, pinking up in the sun. This trip alone would be a reason to quit my new job. But I need it. And a hotel castle deep in the mountains has been exactly the escape I was looking for.

Until the "new employees' outdoor adventure."

The man has extracted a roll of duct tape and rips off a strip with his teeth. He walks backward and holds it out so I can take it without him turning around.

Even with him facing away, I spot his rather impressive member dangling between his thighs as he stands there.

Blood rushes to my spine-infested parts. Damn it.

"If a woman screams on a mountainside and no one

hears, did she really pull a half-dozen needles from her nether regions?" I ask.

"I'll hear you," he says.

I peer down, aligning the silver tape so that it covers all the needles. I'm not bald down there, although I keep things trimmed. Bigger than a Cheez-It, smaller than a Triscuit. Even so, there's going to be some hair coming out with the spines.

I press down, sucking in a breath at the hot flare of pain as the tape pushes the needles farther into my skin.

It's time to pull. I grasp the end, ready to get it done.

And I can't do it.

I clench my jaw, trying to force my hand to obey.

But it won't.

Great. Now I'm sitting in the dirt, two feet from a bronzed stranger, with duct tape for underwear, spines in my girl parts, and I can't even finish the job.

Tears prick my eyes. This is too much.

I shouldn't have had to leave my life in San Diego.

I shouldn't have had to take a job at a hotel when I have a degree in engineering.

I shouldn't have had to change my number, erase my online footprint, and go into hiding.

But here I am.

I can run from my old life, but I can't run from these spines.

"You okay?" He's half-turned, but not quite looking at me.

"Trying to figure out how to force my fingers to yank this off."

He nods. "It's like jumping out of an airplane or

taking off in a hang glider. You have to clear your head and *go*."

"I don't do any of those things." I'm sure he does. He strikes me as a risk taker.

"I can do it." He gestures to his body. "I obviously don't have any hang-ups about being naked."

Of course he doesn't. He's a perfect specimen of a human.

"Let me try one more time."

"Okay. Let me know."

I refuse to have some complete stranger — some completely naked stranger — yank duct tape off my parts. I clear my head like he said, grab the loose end, and jerk.

A scream the likes of which I've never heard come from my body echoes off the mountainside like a horror movie special effect. I suck in a breath, then pant through it. The sting is unreal.

But the duct tape is filled with needles and hair. I look down. I'm red and swollen, but seem to be cactus-free. I press my fingers along my skin. No additional pain.

I got it.

"Did it work?" he asks.

"I think so." Now that this is done, I scramble into my underwear, grimacing at the dust. Once I'm partially covered, it's easier to stand up and go through my back-pack, extracting the shorts.

He waits through all this, hands on his hips, chin lifted to the sky.

When the shorts are on, I say, "I'm decent."

I guess we've both forgotten that he's not, because he turns around and there he is again, all parts of him.

We both look down at his junk. "Right. Sorry." He slides his backpack down and around, covering his front. "Technically, this is my private property. I like hiking naked. I didn't expect to see anyone."

I glance around. "Why would my boss bring me here if it's your property?"

His eyes bore into me. "Your boss brought you here?"

"Yeah. Havannah Boudreaux-McDonald. This is the new employees' outdoor adventure. And here I thought hazing was illegal."

He rocks back on his heels. "I know her. I didn't realize they were doing hikes. This is pretty far afield. Where did you set out?"

"I have no idea. We rode in the back of a big safari Jeep, and they dropped us off at the end of some dirt road. I got separated from the group."

He nods, frowning. "I know exactly where you're talking about. I can get you back."

I glance down at his backpack. "Like that?"

"Right." He sets it down, and there it is again. Mr. Schlong. It's hard not to stare.

He pulls out a shirt and a pair of biking shorts. "Sorry."

I turn around to let him dress as if I haven't already seen every square inch of him. "I'm the one in the wrong place at the wrong time."

I listen to the sounds of him pulling on the clothes, then zipping his pack. "I'm decent," he says.

I turn around. "Thank you for helping. People like me don't do well alone in places like this."

He nods. "It's fine." He looks down at the strip of duct tape. "You want me to get that? We shouldn't leave trash."

I snatch it up, shoving it into my pack. "I've got it."

He shoulders his pack. "All right. Let's see if we can get you back on your trail. You okay to walk?"

"I can walk."

He takes off across the rocky path, and I fall in behind.

It's not even that far to the clearing where the covered Jeep waits for us. The driver jumps off the hood, dropping a cigarette to the ground. "You made it back!" He looks between me and the man who brought me here.

"I did." I turn to thank the mystery man, but he's already disappeared into the brush.

Huh.

The driver gets me a bottle of water and radios the group, who have been frantically looking for me. We assure the others that I'm unharmed and waiting at the Jeep, and I look into the trees, wondering if I'll catch another glimpse of him farther up the trail. I don't.

I can picture him. I might have memorized every muscle of his back and am keenly aware of the swing of his junk.

But I never learned his name.

3

AXEL

By the time I make it back to my property, I've lost my interest in today's hike.

I don't like that I was spotted. Naked hiking might be a thing, legal in all the national forests, celebrated on National Naked Hiking Day in June, and certainly just fine on my private property.

But I don't like it. It's something I do for peace and nature.

And that's blown up in my face.

The woman I startled is obviously not from Colorado, not outdoorsy, and easily spooked.

But she's tough. She yanked cactus glochids out of a sensitive area in the middle of a trail on the side of a mountain with duct tape.

In front of a total stranger.

A naked stranger.

Ugh. If my siblings find out about this, they are never going to let me live it down. They always tell me my dumb habit, as they call it, will bite me in the ass.

It did today.

My cell reception is spotty, so I switch to satellite and call my cousin Anthony. He's in the middle of setting up a combined Pickle and Tasty franchise deli in the castle, and talks to Havannah most every day.

I want to get to the bottom of this bizarre new employee activity she did, why it got so damn close to my side of the mountain, and how the hell they lost someone so clearly unable to manage herself alone on a hike.

Anthony's voice is a question when he answers. "Axel?"

"Hey, cousin. You at Havannah's castle?"

"Just left there. Driving back to Boulder. What's up?"

I hear the wind noise. He must have me on a hands-free speaker. "Is Magnolia with you?" I don't want Havannah's sister to get all defensive while I'm talking to Anthony.

"Nope. Only me. Is something wrong?"

"I took one of the castle employees back to a base camp at the end of that logging road between our prop-erties. When did they start forcing their people on hikes?"

"I don't think they force them."

"I don't think this one had any interest in it. She must have felt obligated. She got lost. She got hurt. And I'm sure she's embarrassed as hell."

"She got hurt?"

"Cactus spines. She had no idea how to handle herself out here. Chickarees threw nuts at her. She thought a mountain lion was after her."

"Aw, geez. You tell Havannah?"

"I called you first."

"You want me to talk to her?"

"You see her every day. How does she take criticism?"

His silence gives me an answer.

"She needs to know," I say.

"I'll mention it to Mags, see what she thinks. Are you saying you're upset she was on your land?"

"Nah. Though I shocked her."

"You were hiking naked, weren't you?"

"Maybe."

"I get it. Havannah won't want to be sued for some unsuspecting employee having to endure a look at your ugly junk."

"Who says my junk is ugly?"

"Every chick who ever saw it."

"I'd put you in a headlock if we weren't on the phone."

Anthony laughs. "I'll bring it up. See where it goes. You want an update?"

"Hell yeah, I do."

"And you want them off your land?"

"That's not the deal. I guess I want her to think about who is running these expeditions, how good they are, and if they're paying any damn attention to where they are going and who's not up for it."

"Got it."

I've said my bit, and I'm about to hang up when I quickly add, "And one more thing."

"What's that?"

"The name of the girl."

"You make a love connection on the mountain?"

"Damn it, Anthony. Just get her name."

He laughs. "What are you going to do about it?"

"I don't know."

"She's already seen your ugly junk."

"Just looking for a name."

He laughs again. "All right. Send her an apologetic card, though."

"Bye, Anthony."

He's still laughing when the call ends.

I shove the phone in my pack and keep heading down the path. Every turn of the trail, every patch of brush, and every prickly pear I pass reminds me of the woman I met.

She probably never wants to see me again, but damn if I'm not strangely intrigued by her.

She's the opposite of my type in every way. I date from the pool of people who are like me — hikers, hang gliders, adventurers. It's not hard to meet them. The last woman I got involved with, I met in a repelling class.

But something about this one has gotten under my skin. And like those barbs on glochids, I don't think I'll be getting rid of the feeling any time soon.

Maybe I'll visit the castle myself.

4

CALYPSO

Someone should create a product called the Hoo-haw Hand Mirror.

It should have a handle that goes at an angle, be long and narrow, and come with its own lighting.

Because using the mirror side of an eye shadow palette to make sure you haven't permanently damaged your bits after an unfortunate cactus incident is next to impossible.

I crank my thighs another inch apart, trying to get a decent view. I don't wear makeup anymore, not really, and only have this palette because my sister told me I had shallow sockets and I better shadow them or be doomed to ugly eyes.

So even though I left all my designer cosmetics behind in San Diego, I kept this one to keep putting a smudge of brown in my crease.

But it's too wide to show me anything useful between my legs.

I sigh and give up, flinging the palette on the bathroom cabinet.

And it cracks.

Great. Seven years of bad luck. Might as well add time to the misfortune I've already accumulated. Maybe I can serve concurrent bad-luck sentences.

I press my fingers along my skin. Nothing seems wrong. It's a little swollen, but that could be the guy as much as the needles.

I can close my eyes and picture every delicious inch.

But thinking about me, spread in the dirt, makes my face flame. I'm sure Mr. Naked God thought I was the greenest city slicker to ever grace his private land.

And he'd be right. My previous hikes in San Diego maxed out on the distance from the beachfront to the port o' potty. We had hills and trails, of course, but I never considered adventuring on one, not for a minute.

I never thought that accepting a job at a castle outside Boulder would entail trudging up the side of a mountain, getting pelted with nuts, and peeing on a cactus.

But I'm done with it. If anything else like this is going to be required of me, I will have to move on. Get my first paycheck and figure out my next move.

I towel my hair dry and slide on a fresh set of clothes. I brought nothing fancy with me to Boulder. No dresses, no heels, no jewelry other than my grandmother's pearl pendant. I needed simple, and I hadn't had time to sort through my things, anyway.

I got out quickly and left anything nonessential behind.

Nobody, not even my parents or my sister, knows where I am. They were always Team Jeremy, anyway. My ex-boyfriend, who refused to accept his position as my *ex*, is probably having dinner with them while they wonder what crazy scheme I've gotten caught up in.

Even if Jeremy has sweet-talked my landlord into letting him into my apartment and spotted the ring box I never accepted in the exact location where he set it down, he's not likely to have told anyone I left it behind.

I fasten the necklace and touch the pearl. Grand-mama was my fiercest ally in the family, and nothing's been the same since she passed.

But she'd tell me to buck up, dust myself off, and look for any bright side to my situation.

And there are several. Living quarters at the castle. A unique and varied job. And distance. Most of all, I'm far away from everything and everyone who made me miserable. Jeremy most of all.

I have freedom.

The light streams in the window. I brush my hair as I stand in front of it, looking out the back side of the castle. Two men are spreading out construction supplies for a pen next to a recently constructed barn. We'll have livestock soon. I don't know anything about that, but I'll get to learn, if I want.

There's an opportunity here. Maybe it's not building bridges or designing roads, but I'll have time for that when the smoke clears. For now, I just need to breathe.

Someone knocks on my door. I've been expecting it. Ever since the hiking incident, I've been waiting for legal or medical or my new manager to show up to talk to me.

I don't think I'll get fired. It wasn't totally my fault I was in over my head on the mountain.

Even so, there will be a report. Or something.

I open the door.

My stomach drops and the nerves kick in instantly. It's Havannah Boudreaux-McDonald, the owner of the castle.

I met her briefly at the new employee luncheon. Her manager hired several dozen of us at once due to the opening of the haunted wing this weekend. Five hundred guests are arriving. It's all hands on deck.

Only after the launch will we get our permanent assignments.

Unless I just permanently lost mine.

Havannah flashes a smile on lips that are perfectly lined with pale peach, which compliments her blond hair. She's in a cream blouse and a dark orange pencil skirt, but on her feet are bunny slippers.

She catches me looking. "I've been on my feet all day meeting with vendors. Sorry for the informality. I wanted to check on you. Calypso, right? Is that what you go by?"

I nod. "I never liked Callie or Cal."

She nods. "Havannah is unusual, and I like it that way. Anyone who shortens it to Anna or Ann is on my shit list."

Her friendly informality sets me more at ease. I step back to let her in.

"You sure?" she asks. "This is your domain, and I showed up unannounced."

"It's fine. I've barely unpacked."

My room is a furnished apartment with an open kitchen, dining, and living area, then a separate bedroom and bathroom. A good chunk of the permanent staff lives on this wing. It's an amazing setup, and I felt so lucky when I first saw it. I really hope I'm not about to lose it.

Havannah perches on the edge of the gold sofa. "How are you feeling? You got left alone on the trail, I hear?"

"I fell behind and lost the group."

She takes me in as if inspecting me for something. "And you got hurt?"

My whole body flashes hot. I didn't tell anybody about the cactus needles. "I'm fine. A hiker found me and brought me back to the Jeep."

"That hiker was Axel Armstrong. He's part of the Pickle family, which my sister married into."

"Oh." So he blabbed. "I'm fine, though. We got the needles out. I don't need to see a gynecologist, and I don't have one here yet, anyway."

"A gynecologist?"

Oh, crap. By the look on her face, I realize Axel didn't specify *how* I was hurt.

"It's fine. Just a poke."

She stands, her face shifting to alarm. "Who poked what?"

Oh, no. She thinks something untoward happened. "He didn't. I mean, he was naked, and I lost my pants, but—"

Her eyes pop wide. "What?"

Oh, God. I've made things worse. "He hikes naked.

I got stuck with a cactus while peeing. He gave me duct tape. He was fine. I'm fine. It's all good." I hold up my hands like I'm trying to ward off any thoughts she might have about this being a bigger deal. I don't want big deals. I need to stay a very small deal.

Havannah presses her hand to her forehead, mussing her perfect wave of bangs. "Okay. Should we get you medical attention? How can I help?"

"I'm fine." I scramble for anything. "I'm tired. Not outdoorsy. So maybe, I guess, if you wanted to help, let me skip the next great outdoor adventure?"

God, I hope she doesn't tell me that if I'm that hopeless in the mountains, maybe I shouldn't *be* in the mountains.

I stammer on. "I love this job. I'm so honored to be here. I can't wait for the big party. I'm waiting for my assignment."

Her expression softens. "It's okay. It's fine, Calypso. We're good. And yes, I'll make sure nobody pressures you to do any of the outdoor events. They are supposed to be optional. I'll make sure they come across that way."

My lungs finally feel loose enough to take in a full breath. "Thank you. Great. Thank you."

She heads for the door. "I'll have the kitchen send up some food. Do you like burgers? Or are you vegetarian? We have great pizza."

"Burgers are great. Love them. Thank you."

When she finally leaves, I collapse back on the sofa. This was one hell of a first week. Orientation was fine. The tours. The team-building stuff. At least until today.

Today was not fine. Not when I found out we were hiking. Certainly not when I got left behind. And then, I got on the radar of my new boss.

But I'm through it. I'm in my room, no stickers in my skin. And I'm getting free dinner.

This isn't my worst day. Not by a long shot.

I have to calm down. Forget the hike, the disaster, the man.

But later, my belly full of burger and the TV turned to Star Trek, where good guys win and there isn't an outdoor scene for eleven more episodes, he keeps popping up in my head.

The bronzed hiker. Naked as a jaybird.

Hung like a horse.

Axel Armstrong.

5

AXEL

To my credit, I let a whole day go by before I drive to the castle to see that girl again.

By then, I've weaseled her name out of my cousin.

Calypso Ash.

I say it over and over in my mind. It's exotic and enticing, the perfect combination of hard syllables and a whisper.

When I pull up to the staff parking lot, Trey, the head of maintenance, lifts a hand in greeting. I'm barely out of my Land Rover when he waves me over.

The morning is chilly, and the wind has picked up, making his gray comb-over flap like a wing. He extends his arm for a handshake. "Axel, just the man I want to see. We could use a little muscle over here."

I glance back at the castle. Its white stone walls with round turrets and two tall towers are achingly bright against the stormy sky. I feel awe every time I see it. I could never have conceived of such a structure outside of Europe.

I'm eager to find Calypso and see how she's faring, but I follow Trey to the new barn. "What's this for, exactly?" I ask him.

"Havannah went to visit the new baby in Avalonia a couple of weeks ago and fell in love with their rare breed of donkey. She's having a small herd shipped here. She thinks they'll be a real draw."

"Donkeys, huh?"

Trey walks us around the side of the barn where a pile of fresh lumber is stacked. "Yeah, she's thinking it'll be a kid-friendly thing. But we need to build the outdoor pens. We could use a hand hanging the gate."

"Sure."

Four men work in the back. Two are digging post holes. One is hauling wood. And the fourth is wrangling a metal gate near the barn wall. This one looks up, his blustery face with a salt-and-pepper beard breaking into a smile. "Hey, you found a victim."

"I did," Trey says. "Vincent, this here's Axel. He's part of Havannah's family."

"I swear everyone around here is Havannah's family," Vincent says.

I reach out to shake his hand. "We're a big brood. What's the trouble?"

Trey heads to the end of the gate. "We need one strong dude to hold this up while we level it."

"I hope I fit the bill."

"You look like it." Vincent drags the gate through the dirt to let me through. "Trey, get those pins and we'll get this done."

Vincent pulls out his level, and Trey positions himself to adjust the pins in the hinge.

I lift the end of the gate. It's heavy all right, but if they get it balanced, it will swing easily.

Vincent sets a level on the top. "Up a little, Axel, if you will."

I brace my legs and lift the gate.

"Down a hair."

It's more work than I figured, holding it exactly in place. I see why they weren't able to manage.

"That's it. Freeze!" Vincent turns to Trey. "Get the pins in."

The breeze has a bite in it, but a bead of sweat pops on my brow as I hold the position.

Then someone exits the barn. I don't have to turn to know it's her. I can tell by the tingling on my scalp. Maybe it's her footfall. Maybe a pheromone. But I'm tuned in to the arrival of Calypso Ash.

"Found the other screws," she says, holding up a bag. She looks totally different today in jeans and a puffy vest over a fitted black shirt. Her short brown hair blows in every direction, and she reaches up to tuck it behind her ear.

Her cheeks are pink, and her eyes are bright. She looks happy.

My grip on the gate slips an inch.

"Hold it in place!" Vincent warns, slapping the level back on the rail.

This gets Calypso's attention. She turns to see what we're doing. When she spots me, she drops her bag of screws and they scatter in the dirt.

"Oh!" She falls to her knees, scrambling to put the screws back in the bag.

"Steady!" Vincent bellows. "Almost got it."

I can't take my eyes off Calypso. Just seeing me threw her off. She went from happy and carefree to instantly ill at ease. Figures. I did see her with cactus spines in places no prickly pear should ever go.

And I was a walking unsolicited dick pic.

This interest I feel for her is probably dead in the water.

"Got it," Vincent says. "Let it go carefully and see if it holds."

I tear my gaze away from Calypso and slowly allow the gate to carry its own weight.

It keeps the position. Trey walks down and gives the end a push. It swings smoothly into the pen.

"Great," Trey says. "Thank you, Axel. Where were you headed?"

To her, I think, but now I hesitate. "Checking to see if Havannah needs help with the big party."

"They could use it," Trey says. "It's chaos in there."

Calypso's still picking up screws. I hurry her way but when I get there, she won't look up at me. She scrapes the screws back into the bag, dirt and all.

"Hey. I can help." I kneel next to her, picking up screws and shaking off the dust.

She doesn't say anything, focused on the ground.

We work silently until they're all in the bag. I wish I'd practiced some opening lines to put her at ease. I should have known she would have strong feelings about seeing me again. It wasn't exactly a casual encounter.

Calypso won't meet my eyes.

I opt for the simple truth. "I drove over to check on you. Are you okay?"

She swivels her head, probably noting the position of the other workers. "I'm fine, okay? Why did you tell Havannah I was hurt?"

Regret thunders down my chest. "I didn't talk to Havannah, but I mentioned you to my cousin Anthony."

Her voice is a hiss. "That I was hurt!"

"I'm sorry. I didn't think you would hide it."

Her cheeks bloom pink and she looks adorable. "Of course I hid it! I didn't want to explain any details!"

This makes sense. "I'm sorry. Very sorry. I just…"

All of my explanations sound creepy, or at least intrusive. I wanted her name. To learn more about her.

"Just what?" she demands.

I'm not getting away without an answer, so I invent one. "I wanted to check on these new hikes she's doing. See if there were more planned so close to our two borders."

"And if they would be on your private property? If you could keep hiking naked?" At the last word, she realizes her voice might carry and checks on the others once more.

I have no choice but to dig in now that I've gone in this direction. "They screwed up on several levels. Too close. Not careful enough. You shouldn't have been on your own."

She frowns. "It's over and done. I have to go. They need these screws."

I look over at Trey and the other workers. They're laying out the lumber in its future locations, which doesn't strike me as requiring screws at this very moment.

It's an excuse. She doesn't want to talk to me.

I'll respect it.

I take a step back. "Glad to see you survived the scrape in one piece. I'm heading in to see if they need any help with the grand opening."

She nods and looks relieved. That tells me all I need to know.

Our crazy introduction means we're doomed.

6

CALYPSO

I'm thrown off by Axel's unexpected arrival at the castle, but he's true to his word and takes off.

I spend the morning helping the maintenance crew build the pen. I get to use at least a small, practical bit of my engineering skills to construct a solid structure with a channel system that will ensure the donkeys don't escape when moved from one section to another.

I wish I'd acted differently when Axel approached me. I don't feel as negative toward him as it probably appeared. It's difficult for me to talk to random people, and here we have this huge, embarrassing moment between us already.

And I don't know him, not really.

Other than what he looks like naked.

I notice the big green Land Rover that wasn't parked near the barn before. It has to be Axel's. It looks like something he would drive.

When we break for lunch, I casually walk beside it to peek into the window to confirm my suspicion.

The front is tidy, with only a Yeti cup in the console and a backpack on the seat.

The same backpack from two days ago.

Definitely Axel's.

There's a wrapper sticking out of a pocket. What does a super-fit daredevil eat? Probably protein-infused plant-based muscle fuel.

But I recognize that wrapper. It's certainly not anything healthy.

It's a banana Laffy Taffy!

Seriously?

I'm a secret lover of Laffy Taffy. The pink ones. I pine for them when they get hard to find.

Imagining bronzed, athletic Axel Armstrong ripping off a corner of yellow taffy with his teeth gives me the giggles, which is exceedingly rare, especially since I left San Diego a month ago. I touch the skin around my mouth. It feels oddly stretched, as if this isn't a position it's taken in forever.

Maybe so.

There is something comical about Axel.

I can picture the Laffy Taffy commercial that would star him. He's on a mountaintop, the wind blowing his hair. He's shirtless, but probably wearing pants since it is, after all, a commercial. He holds the artificially yellow Laffy Taffy in his fist and takes an aggressive bite.

"Laffy Taffy," he says while dramatic-energy chords play in the background. "The right stuff for hitting the trail."

Now I'm losing it. I mime the commercial, me

playing Axel with his Laffy Taffy prize held in the air for the close-up product shot.

I catch my reflection in the window glass. I haven't seen that laughing girl in a long time. The permanent crease between my eyebrows is scarcely noticeable.

This was a good move. Despite having to ditch everything, I made the right choice. Sometimes the only real course of action is to escape.

But then I see something else in the reflection.

Another head of hair, a good foot above mine.

Oh, no.

"Something in my car must be hilarious." His low, rumbly voice is so close, I can feel it in my chest.

He's not touching me, but his body blocks the wind, making me instantly warmer.

"I, uh. Oh."

Articulate to the end.

He cups a hand over his eyes and leans over my shoulder to peer in. "Are you and my backpack having a torrid affair? I mean, you just met, but Blaze is known to fall in love at first sight. I've warned him about it."

"You named your backpack?"

"Trailblazer. Blaze for short. Is it weird?"

"A little."

He lowers his hand. "People name their cars."

"Have you?"

"No. I use my backpack more than my car."

I tap the windshield. "But you drove over here."

"It's a fifteen-mile hike."

"That's pretty far." Talking to him is easier now that we have an actual topic.

"I mean, I can do it."

Does he think I'm questioning his athletic prowess? "I'm sure you can."

"Do you have a car?" he asks. "Does it have a name?"

"No."

That's a lie, because I do, back in San Diego. I couldn't bring it here. My mother traced it once using OnStar. She had a lawyer force customer service to give Mom my location. I canceled the service afterward, but I bet she could get it re-activated for another trace. It's why I left my phone as well. Money can make most anything happen.

No credit cards. No electronics. Just the cash I could pull from an ATM before I left town.

Axel peers through the window again. "Do you think the car is jealous that the backpack has a name and he doesn't?"

"How do you know the car is a he?"

Axel steps back to take in his Land Rover. "Good question. I guess it's the boxy lines. The color. The headlights have a sort of angry look, don't you think?"

We walk around to the front. He's right. The grille and lights give the impression of a face, and it's not friendly. "Yes, I'd say go with male."

"What would you name him?"

"How old is he?" I ask.

"About a year."

"Do you like human names?"

"I'm good with any."

This is the oddest conversation I've had in a while,

but then, so was the one about using duct tape on my tender bits. "I'd go with Frank."

"Frank, huh?" His grin is disarming. "I like it. Frank and Blaze. We sound like a superhero team."

"I don't think there are any superheroes named Frank." I lean against the front of the car.

"Then we don't have to worry about infringing on trademarks."

That's an interesting direction to go. He must be in business. "Axel, what do you do other than hike naked and wrestle livestock gates?"

"You know my name!"

"Because you outed me to my boss."

His eyebrows draw together. "Right. That again. I am sorry. I was just…"

The moment is spoiled. Our easy camaraderie is gone.

I take a step back from him. "It's my lunch break. I need to go eat."

"Can I buy you something? A sandwich?"

"The deli hasn't opened yet." The Tasty Pickle is slated to open its doors after the Haunted Ball. I'm looking forward to it. The other food at the hotel has been a little fancy. Even my free burger was gourmet.

"There's a restaurant." He's so eager. For what? Me?

Getting involved with someone is literally the worst thing I could do. I have way too much unfinished business back in San Diego. I need to get on my feet. Make some money. Figure out what to do with the rest of my life.

"I can't. I'm sorry." I back up a few more steps.

He frowns. "Okay." His frown deepens. "Okay."

He stares at the ground, and I take this opportunity to hurry away. Maybe he's a bronzed god. Maybe he's some athletic girl's dreamboat.

But right now, he's an obstacle in the way of my goal of peace and quiet and invisibility.

I have to avoid him.

7

AXEL

I intend to stay away from the castle. I really do. Clearly it's not going to work out with Calypso. I took my shot and missed by a mile.

But a woman named Lady Pendragon calls me the next morning in a panic.

"Is this Axel? Axel Armstrong?"

I tug on my hiking boots. I was about to head out for today's trail when she called. "Yeah."

"Havannah Boudreaux told me to call you."

I set my foot down, the boot untied. "What's wrong?"

The woman's voice is high-pitched and frantic. "It's a real disaster. She said only you could help."

I snatch up my car keys, shoes untied, ready to race to the castle. Thankfully I'm dressed, since it's cold out. "What's going on?"

"We don't have anyone strong enough to be the ghoul in the Haunted Ball Spooky Spectacular!"

I halt and pull my hand back from the doorknob. "The what?"

"Tomorrow night is the big Haunted Ball at the castle. I'm casting the Spooky Spectacular, and apparently my ghoul is more of a ghost! No one can get hold of him, and no one else in the cast can play the role!"

I have a feeling I'm not going to like where this is going. "What role is that?"

"The ghoul has to carry the princess out of the ball. It's a key moment in the play! I understand you can lift an average-sized woman."

"I can."

"Fantabulous! Please be at the castle at four o'clock for costuming and the first rehearsal. You can make that, right?"

"I suppose so." I'll have to avoid Calypso.

"And be there all day Friday?"

That's more than a rehearsal. "All right."

"Good, good. Come early to the castle to get settled. All the cast will stay on site to make it easy to attend. You'll have a room. We'll provide meals."

Oh. I have to avoid Calypso for two whole days.

"Axel?"

"Yeah, okay."

"Good, good! I'll see you later today."

She ends the call.

I have a ticket to tomorrow's Haunted Ball, of course. Havannah invited the entire Pickle clan and most of the family is flying in for it. I'm looking forward to seeing my brothers, Court and Rhett. My sister is in college and has class, or she'd be here, too.

I won't be able to pick up my brothers at the airport, though, not with rehearsal. Havannah really roped me in on this.

I kick my hiking boots off and send my brothers a quick text to tell them to get a ride to my place. My day is spoken for. No hiking, dressed or otherwise. Time to pack a bag.

When I make it to the Grand Ballroom where the Haunted Ball will take place, I see Trey was right yesterday. Everything is in chaos.

One crew is setting up tables and chairs. Another is decorating the sides of the stage. People are scattered all over the place, sitting against the wall, surrounded by bags. A few others strut around in costumes. I spot a king and a vampire.

At least I hope they're costumes. One of the Pickle cousins married an actual royal prince a couple of years back. So, you never know.

Calypso isn't here. Havannah neither. I don't know a soul.

A woman with orange hair and an oddly witchy green velvet dress spots me and hurries over. "You are a real brute. You must be Axel."

"I am."

"Lady Pendragon." She squeezes my upper arm with utter disregard for my personal space. "Oh, you are a strong one." She gives a hop of excitement. "Come with me for costuming before the director starts organizing everyone."

"Who's the director?"

Lady Pendragon waves toward a tall brunette who is talking animatedly with a trio of women. "Camille. The tall one."

I nod and follow the swish of her green dress. In the staging room to the right of the ballroom, several circular racks have been set up, all filled with elaborate costumes. A beefy man is being fitted with a red coat by two women with pin cushions on their wrists.

Nearby, a young man with a smug expression inspects an old-fashioned gray suit while a young woman tucks a pile of red and purple hair beneath a huge white wig.

"Here's your ghoul," Lady Pendragon tells a woman sorting through more gray suits on the rack. "Will you have tights to fit him?"

Tights? Nobody said anything about tights.

The woman peers up at me. She's got a pencil stuck through the messy bun on her head and wears all black, like stagehands do. She whips out a measuring tape and encircles my thigh. "Nope."

I'm relieved to hear I won't be forced into them, but she dashes my hopes. "Arlene! Send Bertie into town to get some double XL queen tights!"

Double XL queen?

Lady Pendragon gives me a fake smile. "You'll be fine. Nobody questions the masculinity of a man like you." Then she's off.

I'm not worried about my masculinity. I'm worried about the itch.

"Off with the shirt," the costume woman says. "Let's get you fitted."

"Here?"

"You want a dressing room with a star on the door?" Her beady eyes give me a hard glare beneath her pencil bun.

I pull off my sports tee. It doesn't escape my notice that the bulk of the chatter dies down.

"Huh. Look at that. You'll do," the woman says.

She pulls a strange collection of wired black strips from a hanger. "This is your costume. Try not to smash it when you sit. I'll reshape you after each rehearsal, since carrying the princess will flatten it."

She lifts it, but her arms don't come anywhere near my head. I duck down, and when I emerge from the hole at the center of the wiry net, I immediately spot Calypso.

She's stopped near the side wall, holding an orange extension cord and a roll of duct tape.

She sees me noticing the tape, and her grimace grows. Right. Definitely the wrong way to keep our interactions light. I think we're both picturing the duct tape on the trail, because our gazes clash with painful acknowledgment.

I want to say "sorry" or ease her upset in some way, but the room is wild with people, and I certainly don't want to shout.

In a minute it doesn't matter anyway, because she rushes on stage and out of view.

"Walk for me, hotshot," the woman says. "I need to see if the wires do their job."

I take a few strides away from her, turn, and go back. The wired strips bounce and float around me.

"Pretty damn brilliant, if I may say so myself," she says. "And I will. We'll take it off until you've practiced with the princess a time or two. Then we'll get you used to carrying her with it." She motions for me to duck down.

Soon I'm free of the contraption and pulling my shirt back on.

I don't know how I get into these situations. Calypso. The ghoul costume. Endlessly the center of attention.

I blame it on being a Pickle.

8

CALYPSO

I can't seem to get rid of Axel Armstrong.

It's just my luck that the one time I get lost on a trail, squat on a cactus, and am forced to remove needles with duct tape, the guy who witnesses the whole thing is someone I'll bump into over and over again.

We finished the pens this morning, just in time for the arrival of the laughing donkeys. They are adorable, miniature in stature, and their soft hee-haw has been about the best thing I've heard or seen since I arrived at the castle.

I wish I could get an assignment with them, but they come with a caretaker, a gray-haired man with a gentle European accent. Instead, I was asked to help with electrical on the stage set-up for the Haunted Ball.

And of course, I no sooner get to the castle than I spot Axel in the middle of the staging room without a shirt.

At this point, I'm fairly sure I've seen him more often without sufficient clothing than with it.

Not that anyone would complain. He literally stopped conversation until some bizarre collection of wired black netting was put on him.

I can't afford to be anywhere near him, no matter how pretty I think he is. A romantic entanglement is not part of my escape plan.

I keep my head down, charge through the room, and hit the stage to tape down an extension cord for a rear projector that will be part of the special effects for the skit.

There's also a comedian, a live band, and several speeches.

I mostly stand in the wings, watching the first walk-through of the skit in case anyone needs something. I'm asked to put down tape to mark the spots where the actors need to stand so they remember where to go.

At one point, I have to stick down a mark for Axel, but I'm careful not to make eye contact.

They're taking a break when I hear someone call my name.

"Calypso, hon, have you ever run a spotlight?"

I turn to see one of the maintenance crew, a spry gray-bearded man who simply goes by Yonder, waving me down.

I strap the roll of duct tape to my utility belt and head over. "Nope. You need somebody?"

He points at two large metal lights. "Those need to go to the lighting booth, but we only hired one spotlight person. The director wants to run both."

"Is the other operator there to show me how?"

Yonder grins. "I bet so. He's a looker, too."

My mind flashes quickly to Axel, but it couldn't be him. He's clearly in the cast. "I'll keep that in mind."

I head to the lights. They are long and black and unwieldy. I stuff one under each arm and start down the stage steps to walk to the lighting booth at the back of the ballroom.

I'm crossing in front of the stage when I spot Axel. He's back in his wired costume and sits next to an outrageously beautiful woman in a gray gown and white wig.

Something ugly spikes through me. I will never look like her. I will never be that at ease with someone like Axel. Their bright laughter strikes me in the heart.

But who's to say he's interested in me, anyway? Sure, he walked me back to the proper trail. And he came over when I dropped the screws. And there was that moment when we named his car. I guess he did ask to buy me a sandwich.

Okay, maybe he *was* interested. And now he's interested in her.

My steps get heavy, clomping on the floor as I angle away from the two of them.

But Axel jumps to his feet, his wired strips flying. "Can I carry one of those for you?"

Right, like I'm some damsel in distress. Even if my arms are screaming, there's a long way to the lighting booth, and dropping one of these expensive lights would likely cost me a week's pay, I have my pride.

"You think I look too wimpy to carry these myself?"

He stops short. I'm not sure what he does after that.

I beeline for the back of the room before I drop one or both of the lights. Only when I've safely made it to the stairs leading up to the booth and can set one down do I look out through the glass to see what he's done.

And he's back to chatting up the gorgeous girl.

I set the first light by the stand at one end of the booth and hurry back down the stairs to fetch the second. By the time I return to the window, the cast has been reassembled, and the director is moving them into the starting position.

The far door opens, and a man enters. He must be the one Yonder was talking about. He's tall, wiry, and looks like he might star in the next Hallmark movie about saving a cupcake shop in a wintery New England town.

His black hair sweeps across his forehead, and his eyes are unnaturally green. They have to be contacts. That color doesn't exist in nature.

He sees me and his grin is instantly disarming. "Well, hello. Looks like it's my lucky day in the lighting booth."

He expertly picks up the spotlight and locks it onto the stand. "Thanks for bringing these up. Strong *and* beautiful."

I'm not falling for it. "They said you needed a second operator up here."

"I do. Camille thought she could do with only one. The other light was just a backup I brought. But now that she's seen the space, she'd like to have two. Have you operated a spotlight before?"

"No."

"It's easy. I'm happy to show you." He picks up the other light and inspects the bulb. "I'm Hank."

"Calypso."

"We'll be spending a lot of time together during the next two days, *Calypso*."

His proclamation sets me on edge. What if I don't want to spend that much time with him?

Hank attaches the second spotlight. "Lighting someone on stage is like making love."

I have to fight back a laugh. "How so, *Hank*?"

He ignores how I mimic his tone. "You must caress them with light, make them beautiful in your eyes. And then the audience will see the artistry of both the actor and your power of illumination."

"I'll keep that in mind."

He leans down to plug in the power cord and flips the switch. A fan kicks on. The light doesn't beam out immediately, and I tilt my head. It's trapped in the casing somehow.

"The bulbs are like women, needing time and atten-tion to warm up before you use them."

Oh, God. I don't think I can handle too much more of this.

His hand flies over various knobs and sliders. "This makes the beam smaller or larger. This one lets the light out, and these control the color of the light."

I've missed half of those instructions. He did them too fast, probably on purpose. When he comes behind me to show me how to aim the beam, I stiffen. Two days will be too long.

Luckily, when he slides the shutter and the light flows

out, it falls right on the director's backside, causing a laugh to ripple through the cast. The sound is piped in through speakers in the booth.

Camille turns to the light as Hank jerks the spot aside.

A headset on the lighting panel squeaks with indignation. Hank picks it up and slides it over his ears, grimacing.

I guess we weren't exactly making love to Camille.

He moves to his light and flips it on, aiming the beam at the royal family on the left side of the set.

My spot is still on the curtains. I want to ask him where I should point it, how big my circle should be. If it should be a color.

But he's obviously listening to someone in the headpiece. He adjusts one of the colored sliders to make his spot more blue, casting a ghostly pallor on the family.

I wonder if I should do that. I'm on my own already. At least I don't have a headpiece to be squawked at.

Except I do. Hank nods at the invisible voice and opens a drawer. He extracts a second headset. He hands it to me wordlessly.

I have no idea how to make that work either, but I can figure it out. I press a few buttons and soon Camille's voice is yelling at me. I can't figure out how to lower the volume, so I push the earpieces high on my head.

"Spot one on the king! Too hot. Add more blue! Why is spot two on the curtain?"

Clearly, I'm spot two. I grasp the handles and aim it at the king as well.

"Spot two on the narrator!"

That's the man in the red coat. I move it to rest on him, grimacing at how the circle bobbles.

"Spot one, add blue!"

Hank adjusts his light, and finally Camille moves on to yell at the sound people.

"Hold it steady," Hank says. "If she asks for a color, move the slider with that color on it. On the top."

I take in the controls. There are sliders with blue, green, yellow, red, and gray stickers. Currently, only the gray one is pushed aside. Or maybe everything but the gray? I wish I could play with it without getting squawked at. But at least I got the narrator. He doesn't move.

When Axel comes out on stage, I find my gaze, and ultimately my spotlight, shifting to him.

"Why is spot two on the ghoul?" Camille is already losing her voice from yelling, so it comes across as gruff and scratchy.

I immediately correct, but realize my narrator is gone.

"Spot two, go down after the narrator says, 'Off with her.' Cast, run it back to when the ghoul kidnaps the princess!"

This time, I hear the line, but I'm unsure how to turn off the spot. I simply kill the power.

"Don't do that!" Hank springs over to power it back up. "It needs the fan to cool it off. Close off the beam until you need it again." He shifts the gray slider to meet the others and my beam shuts off.

"What is happening to spot one?" Camille shouts.

Hank rushes back.

I'm already exhausted, and it's only midafternoon.

This is going to be a long day.

9

AXEL

I might be used to strenuous hikes, but sitting around all day waiting on my moments during rehearsal wears me down.

I'm glad to be stuck, though, because it keeps me from wandering the castle like a lost soul, hoping for a glimpse of Calypso. I ought to let it rest, but there's something about her I simply can't shake.

Maybe it's how tough she was walking the trail after a traumatic duct tape incident.

Or the way we laughed about naming my car Frank.

Maybe it's how she never smiles otherwise. Every time I spot her walking around the castle, she looks mad or miserable.

It's irrelevant, because once she passes me with the spotlights, I don't see her again all day.

I do, however, befriend Indigo Flame, a social media influencer who is playing the princess I have to carry out of the ballroom. She's funny but distracted. She admits she is meeting someone later and is excited to see him again.

Good for her. At least somebody's getting lucky in love in the castle.

Havannah arrives to watch the rehearsal and sits next to me to wait for the next run-through. "You okay, tight boy?" She pulls on the black nylon I was forced into after the costume coordinator found some double XL queen black tights.

"No ridiculing the ghoul who is saving your play." I nudge her shoulder.

"I'm grateful. And especially thankful that you got my new hire back safely. It shouldn't have happened."

"Glad to do it."

"I'm killing the hikes for the time being. It's gotten cold, anyway."

"Not likely to be any more warm days until spring."

She nods. "I grew up here. You didn't, though, right? All the Pickles are from New York?"

This again. "Technically, I'm not a Pickle, since it was my mom's sister who married into the Pickles. But you know Uncle Sherman."

Havannah drops her voice low to mimic him. "Every Pickle's a Pickle!"

I chuckle. "Nice one. How is the deli looking?"

"Good. The appliances have been delivered. Yonder and Calypso are going to install them once the Haunted Ball is over. Then I have to assign which staff goes where. I have a lot of new hires."

My belly flips at her name. "What is Calypso's job?"

"Technically, she came in as a general all-purpose

employee who could go anywhere from housekeeping to restaurant staff. But it turns out she has a degree in civil engineering."

I sit taller. "She does?"

"Yep. She didn't disclose it on her application, which I find odd, but it came up when my HR person checked references. We hired her, of course, and I'll keep her in the general staff pool. I'm not going to out her unless she wants to be."

This is a puzzle. "She was carrying screws to the builders yesterday."

"The pens were her design. She reallocated the lumber to create a set of interlocking channels that both maximized the space for the donkeys and help prevent any escapes. She's smart. There's something going on with her, though."

"Any idea what?"

Havannah shrugs. "Some people come to the mountains to figure things out. As long as she does her job, I'll let her work on that." She smacks my knee. "Keep your clothes on around her. Now that you're officially doing work for me, I don't need your dangling bits getting me into an HR mess."

"Strictly clothed, boss." I cross my heart over the crazy wire strips.

The lights come up on stage and we go quiet. It's rehearsal time.

The ballroom chandeliers are dimmed, so the waiting cast is bathed in darkness. The spotlight appears on the closed curtain, and the narrator steps out in his red coat to begin the story.

Camille yells, "Spot two, let him come out before you turn on your light!"

The actor has only said three words when the spotlight shakes and sputters.

Camille shouts in the darkness, "Spot two! What is going on?"

I turn to look up at the lighting booth. Normally, the glass is dark and impossible to see through, but this time, the figure of a man clearly walks across to another figure.

The second one is Calypso. I just know it. I can feel it. The two of them hunch over the spotlight. A sudden glow illuminates both of their faces in the dark. I'm right. She's running spot two.

After a moment, the beam of light goes out, then back on again, solid and smooth.

Camille shouts, "Return to opening marks!"

I keep my eyes on the booth. The soft light goes out, and Calypso is only a shadow behind the glass. But at least I know where she is.

Havannah's voice is quiet beside me. "Somebody's got it bad."

Don't I know it.

The production breaks for dinner. I shuck my wired costume and stand in line with Indigo and her friends Drag Scream and Zerobia, but I keep my eye out for Calypso.

"Your friend is distracted," says Drag Scream, who wears a long, black velvet robe. She has a singing part in the production.

I spot Calypso entering the room, and every muscle

in my body goes tense.

"And there's the distraction," Zerobia says. "The big hunky man likes a little slip of a woman."

Their conversation is only in the peripheral of my attention. All my senses are trained on Calypso. She seems agitated and maybe a bit tired. I want to talk to her, ask how it's going in the booth. Ask why someone with her qualifications is in the general staff pool at a castle hidden in the mountains.

My interest is bordering on obsession.

She gets in line at the end. I can't stand it. "Excuse me," I say to the others and take off to the far corner of the room. I circle the costume racks and approach the food line from the opposite direction, watching to make sure Calypso doesn't spot my ridiculous maneuver.

I chide myself the whole time, telling myself to leave her alone. But my feet keep walking, and a minute later, I'm in line behind her.

She's staring at her phone, so it takes a moment for her to notice me. When we move forward, she must catch me from the corner of her eye, because she turns. "And here you are."

"Here I am. Frank thanks you for his name."

"He told you that?"

"He did."

She holds my gaze for a moment. "I guess I'll have to get used to you being around."

"Is it too terrible?"

She hesitates. "I don't think I can hate anyone who eats Laffy Taffy."

I almost take a step back. "How did you know?"

"I saw it in your backpack. Is banana your favorite?"

This is great. "I'm an equal-opportunity Laffy Taffy aficionado."

"You only had banana with you."

"I have cases of them at my house."

She shakes her head. "Cases?"

"Tell me your favorite."

"Pink."

"Strawberry or cherry?"

"Either. Just pink."

"Can I bring you a pink tomorrow?"

We move forward with the line. Her gaze holds mine. "Is there any catch to this pink Laffy Taffy?"

"I mean, I could bring you the rope ones."

"You have the rope ones? Those are rare."

"So you like ropes." I try to hold back the mischievous grin, but I know it's there.

She narrows her eyes. "I like pink."

I like pink, too, but that's my thirteen-year-old boy brain talking, and I'm not letting that come out of my mouth. Although now every thought is centered on her wrists in ropes and everything pink *in* my mouth.

Shit.

"You okay?" she asks.

"Yes. Perfect. Pink it is." I wrangle my thoughts back into the moment. "How are you with mystery swirl?"

She tilts her head. "What are you talking about?"

"The Laffy Taffy mystery swirl flavor. You don't know what you're going to get."

"Is this like the mystery Dum Dums where they use up all the extra flavors and glob it on a stick?"

"I'm not familiar with their methods, but yes, there's more than one Laffy Taffy flavor in the package."

"That's sacrilege."

A chuckle escapes. "So, no mystery swirl."

"You can't talk about it without bringing it!" Her eyes are bright, and I see a glimpse of that happy side of her from yesterday.

"Pink and mystery. I'll have them tomorrow." I'm supposed to spend the night here, but I'll do whatever it takes to get that Laffy Taffy to the castle for another excuse to talk to her.

We make it to the sandwich line, and she looks over the choices. "You better. Nobody likes a tease."

I want to quip about never being a tease, but wisely keep it to myself.

"One more question," I say. "And it's important. Make or break."

"Lay it on me."

There goes my teen boy brain again. "How are you on the jokes? Is the laffy the more important part of the taffy experience?"

"Not big on the jokes."

I cover my eyes in anguish. "Say it isn't so!"

She laughs and my damn heart practically soars. "For you," she says, "I'll endure the jokes."

I drop my hands. "Compromise. I like it. We can be friends."

She picks up a sandwich and chips and gives me a wave as she hurries back to the lighting booth.

I watch her go, a good, settled feeling spreading

through my chest because finally, something is going right with her.

If it takes Laffy Taffy to make her smile, then I'll buy the whole damn company.

10

CALYPSO

The day of the Haunted Ball is absolutely insane. I wear black jeans and am given a black haunted staff shirt with long sleeves and a hood.

I watch the final rehearsals, trying not to obsess about Axel. It's clear he's friendly to everyone, and doesn't spend any more time with the gorgeous princess than the rest of the cast.

At least other than when he's throwing her over his shoulder.

Because of additional acts that I also have to light, I don't have time to see him when the actors break for lunch. So, we haven't had our Laffy Taffy moment.

Hank and I are brought burgers in the booth, and we eat with one hand while using the other to follow our marks on stage.

I like the job. It forces concentration, and creating the perfect symmetry of light and actor makes me feel accomplished, like I've been a part of something artistic. It's a far cry from my old engineering tasks.

As the day progresses, the chaos slowly shifts to order, tables set up throughout the space. A dance floor is laid down. Stations along the walls have art and even a haunted mirror that seems to astonish everyone who stands in front of it. I watch them from the booth, wondering what they see.

Eventually, the band comes on stage to rehearse. They don't want spotlights, so I get a break.

The play cast has moved to the back for hair and makeup, and only waitstaff and decorators are in the ballroom, busily finishing up their work setting the tables.

I head toward the haunted mirror to see exactly what it does.

A server is already in front of it, holding an empty tray, so I wait near an arch filled with black and purple flowers, pretending not to watch.

The mirror fills with gray smoke, but it's not actual smoke, just an illusion. When it clears, the woman gasps and presses a hand to her stomach. "Dios mio," she whispers and dashes away.

I walk up to it. Her reflection is there, but there is a baby in her arms.

Whoa. Based on how she reacted, did this mirror know she's pregnant?

How does it work?

Another server passes by. "Be careful with that. It's a truth bomb."

My ordinary reflection fills the glass. I look tired, and quickly brush down a wayward hunk of hair that's sticking up over my ear.

The mirror fills with smoke. Is it going to tell my future? Or my present? My belly quivers.

When I return, I'm not wearing black anymore, but a long red gown. There's movement behind me and someone appears.

It's Axel.

What?

I spin around to look at him.

But he isn't there.

When I return to the mirror, I'm back in my black jeans and shirt.

What the hell?

I'm tempted to try it again, but two giggling servers rush up for a turn. I back away, watching as one of them steps in front of it. When the smoke clears, she's wearing a tiara and a sash.

"I told you that you were going to win!" the other woman says and shoves her friend aside.

The first one stands open-mouthed in shock. "How did it know I do pageants?"

The second woman stares at the mirror. "I heard it's artificial intelligence. It searches the internet for any public records and morphs an image based on the information it collects. Jana Sparrow did it, and she's not on socials. Very little online footprint. So it showed her in a pirate outfit, like she was Captain Jack Sparrow from the movies!"

"It knew her name?"

"It must have matched an image somewhere. Probably the employee site here. Pair that with a million hits on the movie, and it goofed."

Interesting. I head back to the booth, thinking this over. It might make sense that the AI found evidence that this woman entered pageants, or even found an old pageant photo to use. And the pregnant woman might have already announced it to her friends, or maybe posted on some pregnancy forum.

But that doesn't explain my red dress. And certainly not Axel.

But I also have only the barest online footprint. When I left California, I shut down every social media account with my name and deleted every app. Still, was there maybe some photo floating out there of me in a red dress? Mother made me go to charity dinners, and of course, I had been a debutante. It's very possible those events have photographs on a society blog. The mirror's AI almost surely uses facial recognition.

That had been a completely different life. One that didn't fit me.

I did like the dresses, though. Just not the pressure or the expectations or the attitudes.

Dinner is delivered to us in the booth, and the final touches are done in the ballroom. It's incredible to watch it come together, and the moment all the hovering candles are illuminated, suspended from the ceiling with invisible wires, the cast and staff burst into applause.

The final rehearsal is done, and it goes mostly according to plan. Then all the lights go down, the curtain is closed, and I'm stuck with Hank in a booth until showtime.

Despite all his speechifying about making love with light on the first day, he's quiet. I don't know if

Camille's unending squawking put him in check, because we've only exchanged perfunctory comments since then.

But now we have this open time to sit and wait. I decide to have a conversation.

"So, are you a lighting person full-time?"

Hank looks up from the chicken pasta we got served for dinner. "Yeah. I work for Damonza Lighting out of Denver. This is a minor job compared to some productions I do. I've done outdoor concerts with a team of thirty."

"Oh, so you're with the people on the light board down below."

He nods. "Yep. I got the follow-spot duty. Not the hardest job, but it is the most noticeable to the crowd if you screw up."

"Why aren't you all using the lighting board up here?" I run a finger along the rows of switches and dials.

"It's new. It hasn't been tested or calibrated. It was easier to bring our own."

Huh. "So you do this professionally, and here I got handed it."

He shrugs. "The narrator isn't hard since he doesn't move. It was supposed to be a static light, but Camille insisted on a spot. You're doing fine."

"Is Camille better or worse than the average director as far as being difficult?" Some of the things she's said to both sound and lighting over the headpiece have made me cringe.

"About average. If this were a bigger production, it

would be worse. She's not very fluid with her directions."

"Do you normally only have two days to get lights set?"

He laughs. "I've done shows where I get one rehearsal to nail it."

Interesting.

Havannah's voice comes over the headset. It's the first time we've heard it.

"All hands, we are opening the doors to the ballroom in fifteen minutes. Lighting and sound, start your pre-show protocol. Thank you, everyone, for your hard work."

Camille comes on next. "Cast, everyone should be backstage for final hair and makeup approval. We have one hour until curtain."

Cast members hanging out in the ballroom move toward the rear exits near the stage. Servers come out to light the candles on the tables.

Hank reaches over to the main board to bring the house lights down. The ballroom is lit only by the over-head hovering fake candles and the live candles on the table. It's a lovely dim atmosphere.

The haunted mirror glows, occasionally smoking over as if to entice someone to step forward.

"Did you do the haunted mirror?" I ask Hank.

He scoffs. "Stupid thing."

"What happened?"

"It showed my ex with me. The AI sucks."

"Oh. Sorry."

That doesn't explain Axel in mine, although the

mirror obviously has a camera. Maybe it picked up on the two of us standing near each other. Did it see something we don't?

The members of the orchestra that will play between acts file in through the side door and take their seats. The house music fades out as they warm up.

The sound of it makes my belly warm with anticipation. Mom and Dad loved taking me and my sister Angelica to the symphony. Even though, as young girls, we inevitably fell asleep during the performance, I loved the experience. The theater was beautiful, and the people dressed in gowns and suits. Mom smelled so good, and I felt like a princess in my outfits.

I liked it less later on, when Mom would insist I sit up straight or lamented my short hair, which couldn't be bound into an intricate, feminine updo like my sister's. She had never allowed me to cut it that short at the hairdresser's, so I did it myself. That was the beginning of all the ways I would disappoint them.

And Jeremy was the biggest and the worst.

I shake away any thought of him and focus on the ballroom. Our spots are off, and without the whir of the fans, it's easy to hear each section as it warms up. The airy flutes. The deep baritones. All the strings in turn.

I sink into the happy feeling.

The guests filter in, dressed in elaborate costumes. There are vampires and mummies and all manner of witches. They float through the room like beautiful apparitions, pausing to greet each other. A few find their way to the haunted mirror and some laugh at its antics.

Others step back, their hands to their chests or covering their mouths in shock.

I'm happy to sit and watch them, imagining their stories, their heartaches, their lives.

"Five minutes to curtain," our headpieces squawk.

Hank nods at me, and we power up the spotlights to get warm. The loud fans drown out the subtleties of the music, but I'm glad I got to hear it for a while. It reminded me of the good parts of my old life.

I'm not even sure how to shape the new. I run my hand over the phone in my pocket. It was one of my first purchases after I left San Diego. I set it up with a new number. My old one sits in my kitchen, next to the engagement ring. No one can get in touch with me.

I sent a postcard to my sister from New Mexico when I spent a couple of days there, deciding what to do next. I said I was safe and on my own for a while. I didn't mention Mom or Dad and certainly not Jeremy.

My sister isn't necessarily on my side, as she became the perfect daughter our parents shaped her into, but she's not the worst.

My headpiece transmits Camille's countdown, and I focus back in. The narrator steps on stage. I open my spot. It hovers on him, bright and steady, and I feel good about this job. My tasks have been varied. I've learned new things.

The royal family comes out and the story moves on. When Axel leaps out in his elaborate costume, the crowd gasps and laughs. He steals the show.

He picks up the princess and throws her over his shoulder. A clever special effect makes it appear that he carries her off into the distance toward a big round moon, but really he moves aside to reveal a projection of their silhouettes in a seamless flow.

The two of them will make their way around the hall outside the ballroom to come in through the back doors.

In rehearsals, they simply went through the foyer, so I'm surprised when one of the stagehands opens the door to the lighting booth. "We're going to have the ghoul and the princess pass through here. The foyer is too crowded."

He'll be here.

I've barely registered that he'll be so close when Hank's spot on the king goes dim.

"What the hell?" He frantically shifts his sliders.

Our headpieces immediately squawk. "Someone get a spot on the king!"

"Move to the king," Hank says, bending over his spot.

The narrator isn't talking, so I quickly shift to the other actor and open the light. My heart hammers. Why would his spot fail now? It's been working all day!

Footsteps clomp up the stairs. Sweat beads on my forehead. I'm trying to hold the spot, but the king walks back and forth as he laments his missing princess then falls to his knees. This is way harder than holding the spot in place.

I sense Axel and the princess arriving. The woman moves on, but Axel hesitates behind me. I want to acknowledge him, but the stress is intense. "Don't even think about interrupting me," I tell him, grimacing at how harsh it sounds.

I don't know if he hears me or what he thinks. I can't take my eyes off the king.

"Okay, let's go," says the crew member leading them. I barely notice them out of the corner of my eye. I'm desperately trying to keep a smooth spot on the stage.

Finally, Hank gets his spot back live. "Fade out, then move," he says.

I do as he says, right as the narrator is about to speak. I fade back in on his red coat.

The moment has passed.

Whew.

"Good work," Hank says.

"Thanks."

Even though there is nothing heavy about holding the spotlight, my arms are screaming. I must have been wildly tense the whole time. I'm super relieved Hank's spot is working, because it's his job to find Axel and the princess as they come in the back of the ballroom and lurch through the crowd.

I feel a flash of chagrin at how I spoke to Axel, but it couldn't be helped. I couldn't look at him. And I'm sure he wasn't going to pass me Laffy Taffy in his costume.

Hopefully, we can smooth it over later.

11

AXEL

I hope to find Calypso after the skit to present the Laffy Taffy, but she has spot duties the entire night. I'm not terribly worried about her sharp response to my appearance in the lighting booth. Clearly, things were going wrong, and she was having a moment.

I hadn't realized I wouldn't get to see her all day. The experience of being in the skit feels incomplete, like talking to her was the only real point.

I'm waiting to turn in my ghoul costume when Havannah finds me and kisses my cheek, thanking me for helping.

"Go change into your outfit for the ball and have a good time. Your brothers are at a table on the left side near the front."

Right. My brothers. I vaguely registered earlier that Rhett and Court had gotten into town and used the spare key to get into my house. The day has been intense.

I head to the room I was given as a cast member. I

share it with the man playing the king, but he's back-stage, reveling in his successful role.

I take a quick shower and change into my tux and vampire cape. I had it made by a designer in Italy. Mostly I wear hiking boots and practical clothes for spending the day climbing rock.

But I can clean up with the best of them.

I don't think Calypso has looked me up. I can always tell when a woman I've met has discovered my history. Some seem overwhelmed, others try to dig their claws in. But they are never neutral about it.

I like that she doesn't know about the app, or the half-billion-dollar sale that means I don't work anymore. I retired at age twenty-four, bought my land, and built a house. I enjoy volunteering more than anything else. I give away a million dollars a year to charities I select. Studying them is the most work I do.

It's a privileged life built on a crazy idea, some coding, and dumb luck. But it draws a certain type of woman if they know who I am. I prefer to get to know them before they learn my background, and Calypso is no exception.

I tuck the Laffy Taffy Ropes inside my suit jacket and survey myself in the mirror. I'm unexpectedly excited about seeing her and looking forward to tonight. Hopefully, she doesn't have duties throughout the entire ball, but if she does, I'm ready to help.

But first, my brothers.

When I head down, I'm in awe of everything Havannah has done to make this an incredibly spooky event. It's an entirely different experience walking into the ballroom as a spectator than being on stage.

The original chandeliers are turned way down and the primary source of lighting is floating candles on invisible lines. The room is filled with circular tables filled with people in elaborate costumes.

The band is finishing their set, a head-banging spectacular of drums and a driving beat with unintelligible lyrics. I wander the tables, looking for Rhett and Court. They're sitting near the front, and have somehow finagled a trio of blonds into joining them. I hope one of those isn't supposed to be for me.

"Axel!" Rhett shouts over the music. "Sit!"

There's no way to do introductions with the noise, so I shake my brothers' hands and nod at the women before taking a seat.

I can't see the stage wings from my spot, and I'm already feeling nostalgic about living behind the scenes. Now I'm a regular attendee.

But the band comes to their crashing finale and exits the stage. The orchestra picks up again as the curtains close, and conversation in the room resumes.

"Axel, the star of the show! You made it!" Rhett claps me on the back. He's an older version of me, or so everyone says, with our wild brown hair and blue eyes. He has his arm around a woman in a sexy witch costume, sparkly black and showing a mile of cleavage.

"Who's this?" I ask.

Rhett grins. "Tabitha. That's her real name. Not her witch name."

Tabitha holds out a hand. "Nice to meet you."

Rhett points at the other women. "That's Argentina next to Court. And then Jessica." Jessica shifts chairs to sit next to me. Her long red strapless gown reminds me of her namesake, Jessica Rabbit. The only nod to the theme of the ball is a tiny red witch hat, so small that it could fit on a cat, sitting jauntily on her cascade of blond waves.

"Hi, Axel," she says, and I know that low purr. It's the sound of a woman who knows exactly who I am and what my net worth is. Great.

"Hey," I say to her and turn to my brothers. "Court, you got in all right?"

"Yeah," he says, tugging in annoyance at the bow tie on his tux. Like me, he prefers performance wear and hiking boots. "Your house is a wreck, though."

Rhett tilts a scotch glass at me. "You, my bro, need a housekeeper."

"I had one."

Court laughs. "Don't tell me. She quit over your slovenly ways."

"She had a baby. I don't know if I'm supposed to wait for her to come back or find a new one."

Jessica chimes in. "You didn't ask her about it?"

"I never see her," I say. "One day I came in early from the trail and there she was with this big belly. I had no idea."

"Call her, you idiot," Court says. "Or hire a service until she comes back."

Rhett elbows him. "Like you know what you're talking about. Your apartment is a black hole of filth."

"Shut up," Court says. "Not everybody has a girl-friend who cleans up after them."

With that, Tabitha abruptly pulls away from Rhett. "A girlfriend?"

"Ex," Rhett says.

"When did that happen?" Court asks.

"A month or so ago." Rhett grimaces and takes a sip of his drink.

"Shit," Court says. "Sorry. I should have kept up."

Rhett shrugs.

I contemplate how little I've talked to my brothers in the last few months. I think all of us are realizing it, our gazes clashing with chagrin.

Tabitha leans back in. "I say we should get another round. Girls, let's get the men a drink."

Jessica turns to me. Great. They *have* been assigned. "What do you drink?" she asks me.

"I'm good. I can get my own."

Jessica gestures to the others. "But we're all going."

"Sure. Okay. A dark and stormy."

She nods, relieved that I'm letting her carry out the same task as the others.

As soon as they're gone, I shove Rhett. "Who the hell are these women? What is going on?"

Rhett shoves me back. "They're just women. Axel. Jesus. We met them at the bar. They were trolling for hotties, and we're their marks. Roll with it."

"I'm not interested." I stare into the light booth. Calypso is surely up there until all the acts are done. She may have spotted me already.

Court leans forward on the table to speak around

our brother. "You've never turned down commitment-free female attention before. What gives?"

"I'm not so sure they are commitment-free." The shadows of two people move around behind the window. There's currently no act while the band breaks down. I should be up there. This is the perfect time. "If you'll excuse me, I have someone to talk to."

I don't give Rhett or Court a chance to argue. I stand and take off for the rear of the ballroom.

You have to exit the space to enter the door with the stairs up to the booth. I slip through one door and pull on the lever of the other. It's locked.

That makes sense. They don't want random people stumbling in mid-show, lost or drunk. The crew member who led us through probably had a key card. There's a typical hotel room card scanner next to the lever.

I knock on the door on the off chance they'll hear me.

The wait is excruciating. If Calypso already saw my table and did the math, she might think Jessica is my date.

I'm about to knock again, sweat popping at my hair-line, when the door opens. It's a man.

"What's up?" He glares at me like I'm an annoyance.

"I'm here to check in with Calypso."

He looks me up and down. "She's working."

I sense a competitive edge in him. Has he been making moves on Calypso all this time? How is she taking it?

But then she appears behind him. "Back off, Hank." She scoots around him on the narrow stairs. "Hey."

Hank holds his threatening gaze another moment, then heads up the stairs to the booth.

Calypso waits for him to be out of sight. "You're dressed."

So she didn't see me at the table with my idiot brothers. "It's not all hiking boots and skin."

She's a couple of steps above me, evening out our heights. She grips the rail, and I swear she's almost smiling. "Long day, huh?"

"The longest." I open my coat and pull out the Laffy Taffy Ropes. "Hopefully this will be a pick-me-up for you."

Her eyes alight at the sight of the candy. "Cherry. Strawberry. And mystery! I feel like I should treasure them forever, but nope. I'm going to eat them."

She rips open the mystery one. It's pink and blue. "Oooh," she says. "Let's both try it."

"Joke first!"

"Oh, all right." She peers at the wrapper. "What did the house wear to the party?" Then she groans.

"What? What did the house wear to the party?"

She groans. "Address."

I clap my hands. "I love it."

She nibbles the end and holds it out to me, still shaking her head. The site of her offering me food she's just had in her mouth about does me in. It's intimate. It's enticing.

I lean in and take a bite.

12

CALYPSO

O h, that was a sexy move.

I don't realize until after Axel has taken a bite of the Laffy Taffy Rope that offering him the same candy I ate from myself was an advanced maneuver for established couples.

But then, given our first meeting brought us the sight of each other's naughty bits, maybe it's not too crazy.

He grins. "Mine's blue raspberry and cherry."

I frown at the package. There's a small blue piece in it. "You took my cherry!"

"Did I now?" Axel's grin is wicked sexy.

Hank coughs from the booth. He can hear every word.

I step down to be closer to Axel. "You can take the blue raspberry. I like my pink." A devilish thrill zips through me to say it.

"I like your pink, too."

Blood rushes to all the good parts. I don't remember

the last time I shared sexy banter with a man. Certainly not Jeremy. He was all about me being the good little woman on his arm.

But I'm free.

Aren't I?

A small part of me sets off a warning bell. This is a rebound. Maybe even a rebellion.

It's not real. It can't be. Not so soon.

But I can't seem to stop myself.

"I guess you would know," I say. A smile I've rarely felt lately creeps over my face. I used to smile all the time. Laugh, even. Then things got so out of whack.

"I *do* know." He's so close I can feel the heat of him even in the tux. His sun-kissed brown hair curls over his ears and forehead. He's ridiculously handsome and decked in a very fancy tux.

Then an explosive, "Thank you for your patience!" blares through the speakers, startling both of us.

"Cal, time to light the comedian," Hank calls.

"I thought it was only one spot," I call back.

"I want you for backup."

I sigh. "Thanks for the candy."

Axel nods. "Do you have to work all night?"

I gulp around a tightening in my throat. "Not all night."

"Can I give you my number in case you want to talk later?"

I pull out my phone and hand it to him. "Okay."

He types the number as the MC introduces the comedian.

When he passes the phone back, I turn to go, but he stops me with his arm. "Hey."

"Yeah?"

"My two idiot brothers invited some women to our table, but I don't have anything to do with it."

I'm not sure why he's telling me that. "Okay."

"In case you see us down there. They have nothing to do with me."

I nod. "Got it."

He exits out the side door, and I climb the steps. I frown at Hank when I get back to my spot, both for making me come back up when I didn't need to and for calling me Cal.

"Didn't know you were making a love connection," he says.

"Just conversation." I set the Laffy Taffy on the light board, resting each package on a row of buttons.

"Those are gross," he says. "Sugar and crap in them."

"More for me, then."

He shakes his head but has to focus on the stage as the MC steps aside. He brings down the spot, then opens it again in the center for the comedian.

I watch the tables. Axel enters the back of the ballroom and weaves through them. He approaches one with two men. He sits down, leaving an empty chair between them.

Then the women arrive, each holding two drinks. They're all model-gorgeous and blond. I frown when one of them puts a drink in front of Axel and sits next to him, leaning in close to say something in his ear.

I'm glad he told me about this. Forearmed with his warning, I easily catch his subtle attempts to lean away. I sense his discomfort.

If I hadn't known, this moment would have thrown me.

Because the girl sitting next to him?

Just like in my haunted mirror prediction, she's wearing a *red gown*.

I'm finally turned loose of my duties late in the evening, once all the speeches are done. There's a small snafu when the artist getting recognized for his work disappears before his work is commemorated on stage. But he turns up later, and we simply run the events out of order.

We finally power down the spots, leaving the fans to run until the bulbs cool. I planned to offer to help Hank carry them down, but the other two operators who've been working the main board arrive to take them.

I check in with Yonder, who dismisses me for the night.

I'm not sure I should go into the ball. I don't have a proper outfit for it, and I know I will feel out of place in my stage crew outfit among the fancy costumes.

I pass a clump of security, including Havannah, talking in low tones. I move to the backstage area, where the crew is putting away costumes.

"Did you hear?" a makeup artist whispers to the

hairdresser. "The princess in the skit is the actual missing princess from Europe!"

Interesting.

The woman who played the queen strolls in from the ballroom. "Can I please keep wearing my gown until the ball is over? It's so lovely out there and this is perfect."

A woman with a pencil in her bun looks her over. "Give me fifty bucks and I'll check yours in last."

"Done." The woman lifts her skirts, pulling down a small purse she's clipped to something. She passes the money over.

When she leaves, the woman in the bun sticks the bills in her bra and laughs. "If she hadn't been so mean, I would have let her wear it for free. It's going to take hours to get all this in the lockers."

I nod as if she's meaning to talk to me.

"Didn't I see you with that big feller, the ghoul?" she asks me.

Earlier today I would have shrugged off her question, but I have the Laffy Taffy Ropes in my pocket. "I was."

"He's out there in a hot tux. I saw him." She smiles and nods at me. "You going out there with him?"

I shrug. "I feel weird going out there like this." I gesture to my black clothes.

She pinches her lips. "I liked him. And he had his eye on you." She moves hangers swiftly on the rack. "I think I have exactly the right thing. I'll let you wear it, if you like. There are some gold slippers in the shoe bin near the back. We keep them for generic footwear. We have all sizes."

She keeps moving the hangers. "Here it is."

When she lifts the dress, I feel light-headed. It's gorgeous, asymmetrical with only one shoulder. It's short in front but long in back, so the hem length isn't an issue for walking.

And just like the other woman sitting by Axel, it's *red*.

13

AXEL

The moment Calypso enters the ballroom in the red dress, it's as if the world stops.

I vaguely register that the orchestra is still playing. Jessica is laughing at something Rhett said.

But I can't take my eyes off Calypso.

There shouldn't be much different about her. Her short hair falls in its thick waves over her ears. She hasn't put on makeup.

But the dress she's wearing hugs her body like a silky second skin. It reflects on her cheeks and neck in a soft blush. The lights dance in her eyes as she glances left and right, walking through the room like she's parted a sea.

I think of Princess Diana, of goddesses and queens. Sculptures and grand paintings aloft in museums.

There's nothing like her. I can't catch my breath.

My chair slides back as I stand. Jessica stops talking, looking up at me, but I only mildly sense her in my periphery. She asks, "Axel, is everything okay?"

Then she turns to see what I'm looking at and says, "Oh."

"Excuse me," I say to no one in particular and head Calypso's way.

She spots me, a small smile flirting with her lips as my feet move with urgency, as if someone might snatch her from me if I don't hurry.

Then we're standing face to face, paused at the edge of the empty dance floor.

"Now this is how you go to a ball," I tell her.

"Hey," she says, then looks down at her dress. "I didn't have a pocket for the Laffy Taffy, so I ate it."

I laugh. "You were supposed to."

"Good." She presses her hand against her belly self-consciously.

I take it and hold it in mine. I haven't touched her before, and the connection is electric. "You look breathtaking."

She looks down at our joined hands, and her throat bobs. Good. She feels it, too. I can only scarcely hope that she put this gown on for me.

"The costumer loaned me the dress. She said it's from a Marilyn Monroe act."

I lift her arm to look at it more closely. "It's perfect."

She presses her other hand to her cleavage. "It's something."

The MC steps out on the stage. "And now, for the 'Moon River' waltz. We invite all you fiendishly fright-ening lovers out there to grab the monster to your left and join us on the dance floor."

I turn to Calypso. "Do you know how to waltz?"

"I did when I was in cotillion at age twelve."

"Same."

"You did cotillion?"

"Mother made me."

"So did mine!"

"I guess maybe they were planning on this moment."

Her expression falls for only a moment before her smile returns. She turns to the dance floor. Several couples have already begun to fill the space. "Let's see what happens."

We step onto the connected squares. I'm not completely confident that I can pull this off. I haven't attempted a waltz in a decade at least.

But when she turns to me and rests her hand on my shoulder, muscle memory takes over.

We take that first step together, and after that, it's like we've danced all our lives. Our feet move easily to the one-two-three pattern of the waltz. The aching melody of "Moon River" flows over us.

Calypso's eyes meet mine, and I'm captivated in a way I've never been before. My entire body feels activated, like I've shot an energy drink directly into my veins.

We glide along the floor, and now that we have the basic steps down, I turn her as we move. The bottom of her dress flares out from her ankles, and her gold slippers whisper on the ground. The movement ruffles her hair, and the highlights in her eyes haven't dimmed a bit.

If music were a ribbon, it would weave between us, surrounding us, and drawing us together. We keep proper dance distance at first, but as the song goes on, we slip closer and closer, until our bodies are one moving part. We cross the floor, easily shifting around the other dancers, at one with the instruments and the emotion of the composition.

Only when the other dancers pause to clap do I realize the song has ended. Calypso and I are no longer moving, but standing close together, gazes locked. The urge to kiss her is incredibly strong.

But the MC blares into the quiet space. "Thank you, waltzers. Everyone else, get your dancing shoes on, because we'll move on with a wild and spooky rendition of 'The Monster Mash.'"

This kills the mood. I take Calypso's hand and lead her away from the dance floor. I can't take her to the table with my brothers. The three women are there, including Jessica, who has slid over a seat to sit next to Rhett. Plus, my brothers are the worst. I'm not ready to subject Calypso to them.

We head into the foyer. There's a good number of people out here, mostly the ones in elaborate costumes wanting to be photographed in the light.

"Have you been on the haunted wing yet?" Calypso asks.

"No. I had to stay with the cast on the main wing, and I haven't wandered the castle since the new one opened."

"We should go. It's open tonight for tours."

I follow her, trying not to stare at the plunging back of the dress or the way the fabric shimmers over her curves. We approach the haunted wing, its doors thrown open. A low voice echoes from overhead. "Enter only if you dare."

"It's amazing," Calypso says, and everything about her is so different from that day on the trail. I'm completely mesmerized by her smile, her exuberance. What sometimes takes these things away from her?

Other than cactus needles.

On our left, an old-fashioned bar is run by a man wearing saloon gear. He turns to watch us pass, and the left side of his face is a mere skeleton. It looks so real that I recoil ever so slightly.

Calypso laughs. "I saw that. Isn't it cool?"

"It is."

"And watch the floor up here."

We continue down the hall, and suddenly, I feel off kilter, as if the earth is moving. "It's a trick floor?"

She nods. "It's intended to make you feel unsettled for when this happens." She gestures to the empty space ahead of us.

I'm about to ask her what she means when a ghost appears from nowhere in the hall.

I take a step back, surprised, then laugh. "That's great!"

"I watched them adjust it yesterday. There's a superfine smoke that allows the projection to work."

"You're revealing all the magic," I say.

"I like the way things are made."

"It's fun to see the wizard behind the curtain."

She nods and we move on.

The floor here has breaks in the carpet, a purple

glow emanating from them. I hear a strange creak, then a cracking sound.

I meet Calypso's amused gaze. I take a step back. The cracking sound is louder, like the floor is about to snap.

"They did this up," I say, then startle when a cool wind rustles a ficus tree by a bench.

"They did. It's one of the reasons I wanted to work here. It's all so inventive."

I'm tempted to ask her where she worked before, but I'm stopped by what Havannah told me. Calypso hadn't revealed that she was an engineer, and some people come to the mountains to figure themselves out.

"What assignment are you hoping for?" I ask her.

"I'd love to do maintenance on this wing," she says, letting go of me to hop forward and make the cracking sounds in the floor louder. "But the maintenance crew is pretty full. I'm installing equipment in the new deli tomorrow, I think, although there's bound to be tear-down duties after the ball."

We pass the various luxury suites and come to the end of the hall. I'm not sure where the doors lead. I haven't wandered the castle much more than during the tour I took when it first opened.

But Calypso pushes through with confidence, leading us to another hall of ordinary hotel rooms. "This circles back," she says. "Then we'll be in the lobby."

"Are there other cool parts of the castle you've discovered?"

She glances left and right, as if making sure no one overhears her. "There's a secret suite."

"Secret suite?"

"Yeah, in the turrets. It's a level the elevator doesn't stop on. You have to know about it."

"You think anyone is staying there tonight?"

"It's possible. The castle is filled to the hilt and there's lots of VIPs."

"They'd be at the ball, though."

Her eyes go wide. "You think we should go in there even if it's occupied?"

"I guess you could get fired."

She presses her lips together. "We could knock first. I mean, I am an employee. I can make any excuse."

"Only do what's comfortable for you."

Her eyes glimmer with mischief. "Let's go."

This is so far from the Calypso I'm used to that my heart actually leaps. We move swiftly down the hall and cross the lobby. Then we take a right into a different wing. Calypso uses her card to enter a nondescript service door.

We enter the staff hall.

"Behind the scenes," I say.

She nods. We arrive at a single elevator.

"I don't remember this one," I say.

"It's the private VIP elevator. It has an unmarked entrance for people who don't want to go through the lobby."

Although I could be a VIP if I want, I never opt for secret entrances or high-end suites. I leave those to celebrities, politicians, and billionaires.

I'm a measly half-billionaire.

Calypso uses her card to summon the elevator. When we step inside, we're surrounded by mirrors. I have incredibly illicit visions of what we could do in front of these mirrors and have to keep myself in check.

Instead, I enjoy looking at her from all angles without having to stare directly at her.

The elevator stops at the eleventh floor.

Calypso moves toward the door. "You have to get out here, and then go down a secret set of stairs."

"If you were on the normal stairwell, would you notice you've taken a double?"

"Maybe, but there's not a visible door."

"Wild."

We exit into a small foyer with two doors. One is marked as the Cinderella Suite. The other is labeled as janitorial.

Calypso opens the janitorial door with her key card.

There's immediately a set of shelves filled with boxes of paper towels and cleaning supplies. They are impeccably organized, but I don't recognize any of the brands. I peer at one.

"Those are fake," Calypso says. She pulls on one to show me they don't budge.

She stares at them a moment. "I have to remember. Yonder showed me." She runs her hands along the eye-level shelf full of Perfection Pillow Mints. Beside them is a bright yellow bucket.

"Right. It's the bucket." She pulls on it and something clicks. The entire shelf swings away from us, revealing a set of stairs.

"Voila." Calypso grins at me, gesturing for me to go ahead.

For a split second, I wonder if I'm about to be murdered by a woman I barely know, but then she pulls the hall door closed and passes me. I decide that if my time is up, my time is up.

Lights pop on as we descend the stairs. The walls are painted in a pastel rainbow, and each wall sconce is an Art Deco-style cloud.

We arrive at the bottom to another door requiring the card. "It opens into a foyer," Calypso says.

We step through and it's literally like we've walked into the sky. The white carpeting is lush and thick. The walls are perfectly blue, brighter on top than on the bottom.

Clouds are suspended from the ceiling by invisible wire, some high, some low. It feels like we're walking among them. I reach out to touch one. It's softer than cotton but as fluffy and white.

"Wow."

"I know, right?"

There's a door ahead. It's marked "Secret Suite." Below it is a plaque that reads, "All who enter here agree to keep the secret."

She turns to me. "Do you?"

"Of course."

We knock on the door to see if anyone will come. Calypso calls out, "Maintenance!"

She peers at me. "If someone's stuff is in there, we'll take a quick peek and leave."

I nod.

She opens the door.

It's clear from the moment we enter that the suite is unoccupied. It has a silent, undisturbed quality.

The first room is an extension of the clouds in the foyer, but themed to sunset. The colors of the walls shift between white, pale pink, and orange. It's filled with pastel furniture, and soft white curtains frame grand windows that look out on the mountains. I can barely make out the snowy peaks in the distance in the dark.

"This is magical," I say.

"There's a kitchen through there," Calypso says, pointing to an archway. "Do you want to see the bedroom?"

Oh, do I.

14

CALYPSO

As soon as I mention the bedroom, I want to pull the words back. It wasn't meant to be an invitation.

But Axel doesn't make any untoward remarks and follows me silently through another archway.

This room is themed like a starry night. I flip on the light, and crickets chirp. There is no direct overhead, only constellations of stars that begin a slow, hypnotic shift across the ceiling.

Everything is bathed in black and midnight blue—the bed, the furniture, a recessed reading nook.

"You can theme the night," I tell Axel. I shift the dial on the wall.

Jungle sounds fill the space, and the colors take on a green tint. There's a rush of wind and the shadows rustle as if majestic trees protect the room from overhead.

"This is incredible."

I turn the dial once more. Now we're aboard a ship, and the sounds are the ocean lapping at the sides. The stars brighten, rocking slightly side to side as if viewed from a moving vantage point. The colors are deep blue and the illusion is so complete that you can almost smell the sea.

Then I realize I *can* smell it.

"It has a scent?"

She nods. "Some settings do."

Axel walks the room. "I like this one best."

I watch him move closer to the bed, so handsome in his tux and cape. I'm acutely aware of his nearness. And how alone we are.

"Thank you for showing me this." He stares up at the stars. "I never knew the castle had so many fantastic details."

"Even the regular rooms have wonderful features. But this is next level."

I remain by the door, unsure what happens next. What am I doing here? Why am I pursuing this at all when my life is nothing but a mess I've left behind?

He quirks a half-grin at me, returning to the door where I've stood frozen. He takes my hand and lifts it to his lips. His mouth is warm against my skin, and I shiver.

"Calypso?" His voice is low and husky.

"Yeah?"

His gaze holds mine. "I've been making excuses to come here and see you. But would you be interested in seeing me outside of work? Somewhere other than the castle?"

I hesitate. The castle is a good half-hour from anything. I don't have a car here. I'd be relying on Axel.

Flashes of Jeremy's lectures and admonishments and reminders of how to act steal my words. It took years to pull myself free. Do I really want to dive right back in with someone else?

"Too soon," Axel says easily. "How about I bring you more Laffy Taffy the next time you have a day off? Would that be okay?"

I nod, grateful that he's able to read me. That's more than anyone has ever done. He already understands and is accommodating without me even asking.

I manage to squeeze out a few words. "Don't steal my cherry taffy next time."

"I wouldn't dare."

We head back to the normal parts of the castle. I think of the night room, wishing I'd behaved differently, wanting to have seized that stolen moment. To have kissed him.

I've learned to be cautious, but I used to be rash. Impulsive. Silly, and a little wild. All that was shamed out of me.

I'm not sure how to get it back.

Axel makes me want to try.

Axel and I dance one more time at the ball. I end up meeting his brothers, who scoot their way near us on the dance floor. The other red-dressed woman has disappeared, and only Rhett and Court have dates.

We barely say hello before Axel steers us away. "I don't want you judging me by those maniacs," he says.

"How long are they here for?"

"A couple of days. When is your next day off?"

"It's been completely random."

"You have my number. Text me when you need a sugar rush."

"Do your brothers love Laffy Taffy as much as you?"

Axel chuckles, and I feel the rumble in my chest. "Good point. I'll hide all the pink ones."

We finish the dance and wander backstage. The bun woman sees us. "Aw, look. My dress is magic. Don't forget to turn it in."

Axel looks at it. "I think it was made for her, don't you?"

She shrugs. "There are lots of pretty women in the world."

I spot Yonder and he waves me over. "Hold on a second," I tell Axel and hurry to my supervisor. "Everything okay?"

"I apologize, but can you come down early tomorrow, like six?"

"Six?" It's after midnight, and it's been a long day.

"I know. It's a lot. But Havannah's family wants to try out the deli before they leave town, and we need to install the ovens and a few other appliances."

I nod. "Sure, Yonder. I'll be down at six."

"Thank you. I promise to get you extra time off for this."

Time with Axel. "Great, thank you."

I turn away to see Axel speaking to the costume director. She looks to be shoving more money in her bra.

"What's going on?" I ask as I approach.

"Lover boy here bought the dress. It's yours. Keep the shoes. I've got a ton of them." She pulls the empty hangers from the rack.

I turn to Axel. "You didn't have to do that."

"Oh, I did," he says. "I couldn't let it go."

My belly flips. "Well, thank you. I can pay you back for it."

"Mmm, I don't think so. How about my payment is I get to decide when you wear it? Maybe sometime down the road. A dinner, maybe?" He grins and adds, "Months from now, of course."

"All right."

He takes my hand. We wander past all the empty racks. Camille's crew pushes the big rolling trunks out to the loading dock. "I don't want the night to end," he says.

"It's been a good one."

"Was that your boss?"

"Yonder is my direct supervisor in maintenance until I get a permanent position." I sigh. "And I've been informed that I have to come down at six to install the appliances in the deli."

Axel lets out a rush of air. "That's not too far away at this point."

"I know."

"I guess you live here on site? I understand that most of the staff does."

"I do."

"Should I walk you to your door? Your wing?"

"The wing is good."

We pass through the kitchens, where bleary cooks are cleaning up. The ball's winding down, and food service has ended even though the bars won't stop serving until one.

The energy has ebbed, although I feel electrically charged, especially as each staff member sees me with Axel and registers surprise.

Right. I've only been here a week and I'm already hooking up.

Too soon. Too soon.

But when we arrive at the outer door to the staff wing and he turns to me, my breath catches. Maybe the timing isn't ideal. Maybe I have a lot of relationship baggage.

But this man is incredible. Gorgeous. Courteous. Kind. I'm not sure he can be for real. And I feel so good with him, like maybe, just this once, life has served something especially suited for me.

So when he squeezes my hand like he's going to walk away without pressuring me for a kiss, I don't let him let me go. I hang onto his fingers.

I tilt my chin and keep my gaze on his.

And by God, if this man doesn't understand me to the core. In an instant, he's bending down, his lips on mine, his hands in my hair.

This is no friendly kiss. It's not Axel's way. He drags me against him, pressing our bodies tightly together. His mouth is eager and seeking. He wants his intention known. He desires me in every way, and he's going to put all that feeling into this kiss.

I register all this in my head, and my mouth, and every part of my body. This time when the heat blossoms between my legs, there is no prickly injury, only the rise of need.

Jeremy never kissed me like this. No one has. Not ordinary Calypso with her short hair and plain face. The one who'd rather not be noticed.

Tonight, I am seen.

His tongue finds mine and they learn each other. His hand spreads wide on my naked back where the dress exposes my skin.

I've done these things before, but they've certainly never felt this way. Kissing Axel Armstrong is a full-body experience.

And even when he finally pulls away, I know it's not one I'm going to forget anytime soon.

"Goodnight, Calypso," he says.

I touch my lips. "Goodnight, Axel."

He strides away with a jaunty step, his hands in his pockets. Just before he turns the corner of the hall and disappears, he looks back at me and flashes a wicked grin.

I shake my head at him, warm from the kiss, then pass my card over the reader to enter the wing.

Somehow, some way, between my disaster in San Diego and this new start, my luck has completely and utterly changed.

15

AXEL

I wake up at dawn as usual, even though my brothers kept me up till three. Those two punks snore away in the guest rooms.

It's a quarter to six, and the sun hasn't quite made its appearance over the mountainside. When you're this deep in the foothills, it can take a while for morning to fully arrive.

It's thirty degrees out, but I step onto the back deck anyway, hot coffee in hand. I'm used to camping in worse weather than this, and the chill helps clear away the cobwebs of sleep.

I rest my feet on the chair next to me, subzero socks warding off the cold. My gray sweatpants aren't only for athletics. They have a heat-retaining layer and a fleece liner.

With my Denver Broncos hoodie and my hands warmed by the mug, I'm fine, just fine. The sky brightens as the minutes pass, and I wonder what morning ritual Calypso has to start her day. She has to report to her boss in seven minutes.

The night went well. Very well. It was worth the trouble of wearing tights.

My brothers and I met up with our Pickle cousins before we left the ball. Jason, Max, and Anthony are hanging around today to get the staff started with the new deli that will open next week. Havannah decided that since the whole Pickle crew is there, they ought to break in the new deli with the founding family present.

Calypso will be there.

My cousins will be there.

Pickle bread will be made.

Hell yeah.

I'm going.

I drop my feet to the ground and head back inside. My lug-head brothers aren't going to wake up for hours. By then I could have spent half a day with Calypso, helping around the new deli, and talking to my cousins.

I pause in the kitchen to grab a handful of Laffy Taffy and sort out a handful of pinks.

I can't go without bearing gifts.

When I arrive around seven, I park in the back of the castle. I know the door that's generally unlocked, and today it's propped open.

A big truck is backed up to the loading dock, the words "Farm Fresh Pickles" emblazoned on the side. This makes me pause for a moment. Pickles aren't farm-fresh. Cucumbers are. Pickles are soaked in jars for days on end.

But marketing doesn't always follow logic.

I scoot inside to an open storage room filled with crates and extra tables and chairs. Several employees unload boxes.

I figure if I follow the pickles, I'll find the Pickles. There are vast swaths of the castle I've never explored, including the pools and weight room, the business area with desks and charging ports, and wherever the new deli is going in.

A man with a "Farm Fresh Pickles" hat hands me a box, and rather than correct his perception that I'm an employee, I simply take it and fall in behind the others taking the produce out of the room.

We go down a hall that leads to a gigantic kitchen. Doors on the right are propped open and lead to a quiet dining area. A breakfast buffet is being set up along one wall.

Two more propped doors lead to the ballroom, and I start to orient myself. Ahead is the staging area where we got costumes, and soon I'm walking the path I took with Indigo after I hauled her off stage.

We make it to the foyer and turn left, away from the lobby and the doors to the ballroom. There's a considerable amount of noise ahead, and a pile of boxes grows as the workers in front of me add to the stacks.

A side door is thrown open, but it's partially blocked by a huge silver appliance covered in a film to prevent scratches. "Over here!" That voice I know. It's Calypso, and she sounds under stress.

I lean through the door to peek around the oven.

"It's a tight squeeze," says the man I remember from last night. He's Calypso's supervisor, Yonder. "We'll have to push it in square or it won't go. We can't use a hand-cart or a roller."

"It's heavy," says a young man who can't weigh a hundred and twenty pounds soaking wet.

I take in the situation. The mega-appliance is a double-wide oven with a second double set above the burners. The industrial kitchen is a small space, with a wood chopping block counter down the center. One wall has sinks and two huge steel refrigerators.

Another wall sports a cutout with a long metal trough filled with empty bins and a sneeze guard, presumably where people walk up to order sandwiches. It looks out over a seating area filled with tables and chairs wrapped in their protective plastic.

Calypso spots me peering around the oven. "Axel?"

"Can I help you move something?" I ask.

The other two men take me in.

"He could definitely help," Yonder says.

I squeeze through the gap. "Does that produce need to go in the fridges?" I gesture to the new round of boxes arriving.

"Probably," Calypso says. "Let's get this in place, then we can sort through all that."

She seems in charge, which I find interesting, since she's only worked here a week. But I smile inwardly. It makes sense. Her skill set is way above her current job. Sometimes it shows.

"I'm Yonder," the older man says. "This here's Joe. Seems like you know Calypso."

I nod. "Nice to meet you. I'm Axel Armstrong. A roundabout cousin of Havannah."

"Ahh, one of the Pickles," Yonder says.

"Sort of."

Uncle Sherman's "Every Pickle's a Pickle" echoes in my head.

Yonder pulls the film from the oven. "We've got a fancy setup here. It's a double oven with a dough proofing box above it. Space is tight, so there's no margin for angling it in."

I nod. Yonder and Joe get the oven uncovered. When the two of them push, I see the problem. It's heavy.

"Let me get this side," I say.

Even with me helping, we're still rocking it side to side to move it.

"Gonna be tough," Yonder says.

He's right. It's a tight fit and once we're close, there isn't room for all three of us to shift it.

"Let's get it good and straight," I tell them. "Then I'll move it in place."

"Don't go all the way," Calypso says. "When we're about two feet out, I need to hook it up. Then you can finish."

It takes several minutes, some grunting and sweat, but we get it aligned. Then Yonder and Joe move aside and I put all my muscle into it. What is this thing made of, granite?

"Okay, stop!" Calypso says. She climbs up on the

counter and bends down behind the stove. I get a nice look at her ass as she hangs behind the oven.

Then her head pops back up. "Okay, ease it in."

My inner thirteen-year-old boy can't stop himself. "That's what she said."

Calypso sits back on the counter to glare at me. "Axel!" But then she laughs. And it's no ordinary laugh. It's a shoulder-shaking, take-over-her-body full-on gut-buster.

Yonder and Joe exchange glances, then the older man busts into guffaws. Joe shakes his head like we're all crazy.

"Sounds like a party in here!" We all turn to see my cousin Anthony. He's quickly followed by Jason, Max, and Uncle Sherman. The room shrinks considerably. Max is a bodybuilder and makes me look puny. Uncle Sherman could stop a tank.

"What are you doing here so early?" I ask him.

"Talk to Dad," says Max. "He insisted."

"Pickles rise early and get a running start on the day." Uncle Sherman elbows Jason, who admittedly looks a little green after the late party. "And he knows his limits."

"Where are the girls?" I ask. All three of my cousins are spoken for at this point.

"The *ladies* are in repose," Uncle Sherman says. "And that is immaterial." He rubs his hands together and looks at the deli space. "This is small, but we can make it work."

"Who says it's small?" a voice booms from the hall.

I strain my neck to look even though I have a feeling I know who it is.

He steps inside, his belly preceding him.

It's John Paul Boudreaux, Havannah's father. He's the owner of the Tasty Pepper, which has a hardcore rivalry with Anthony's Pickle franchise. He's not Uncle Sherman's favorite person, even though Anthony married John Paul's other daughter Magnolia, making them family.

Havannah herself peeks over her dad's shoulder. "Daddy, don't talk trash about my new deli." She squeezes past him.

Now there's ten people in the space meant for a small crew. Havannah runs a hand along the controls. "Oh, good, you've about got the oven in. Isn't it great? I had it built special to save space."

"Calypso hooked it up," I say. "We just have to push it in."

I know better than to add, "That's what she said." Uncle Sherman already admonished me once.

But it doesn't matter. Everyone talks at the same time, discussing the optimum placement of the trays in the counter, and if the dishwasher shouldn't be somewhere else.

Then Anthony asks me about my brothers, and the room practically booms with conversation.

So much for time with Calypso.

16

___

CALYPSO

I hop down from the counter and move farther into the kitchen. This is too many people for me, and all of them are incredibly intimidating: deli chain owners, franchisers, my head boss, and my supervisor. My chest feels tight and my stomach is acting like I ate something that expired last summer.

Axel is busy shaking hands with the other men. He belongs with them. He has the same easy confidence, that sure knowledge that he belongs.

I've never known that feeling, and being in the midst of so much of it is like watching all the high school cliques laugh together in the cafeteria as you try to figure out where you can sit. The last thing you want is to attract the attention of anyone who might point out what an outsider you really are.

I want to get smaller, to curl into a ball. I back up so far that I wind up next to the door of the supply pantry and realize there are boxes inside that can be unpacked.

So, while everyone is talking and laughing, two of

the men pushing the oven the rest of the way in, I dart into the pantry and away from the heat of my discomfort.

The noise level rises as multiple conversations compete in volume. I partially close the door to cut it down. My head is pounding from the overwhelm.

I focus hard on arranging jars of pickles, relish, and salsas, mostly in the Pickle brand. Then there's bags of flour and sugar. I stack them low.

The work is easy and monotonous, which soothes my overstimulated system. I realize I got lucky yesterday with the lighting booth. Other than creepy Hank, I was away from the crowded bustle of the show.

I've almost finished with the boxes that are already in the pantry when Anthony Pickle pokes his head in. "Hey! Calypso, right?"

I nod.

"We have a lot more boxes. Are you going to be in charge of unpacking?"

Havannah comes in behind him and takes in the shelves. "Hey, she's good at this. It might be nice to have a third party arrange things rather than have Dad and Uncle Sherman fight over the arrangement."

She must summon the beasts, because both of the older men peer in.

"No, no," says the man that Havannah called Dad. "Always put the jars in the very back. You'll need them the least. Bread ingredients in the front, where they can be picked up easily each morning."

"No," booms the other man. "All baking goods in the back because you only need them once a day."

Havannah's dad immediately retorts, "Maybe you don't sell enough sandwiches in a day to need to bake bread more than once."

Sherman shoots right back, "Maybe you don't plan properly in the mornings to make enough bread to last the day."

Havannah raises her voice in a way I've never heard her do. "Dad! Uncle Sherman! Stop! You're going to scare off one of my star employees!"

Star employee? Does she mean me?

Sherman clears his throat. "She's doing a fine job."

Havannah's dad sighs. "It's very logical, putting the heavy things on the bottom."

Havannah pulls both of them back. "Sorry, Calypso. I'll have the brothers stack the dry goods near the door for you to unpack. Thank you for hooking up the oven. We're about to test it."

"With the finest Tasty Pepper bread," her dad says, moving into the kitchen.

"I thought we agreed it would be the dill dough," Sherman says.

My head pops up. "The what?"

Axel peers in. "Aren't the names great?" He shoves two boxes into the pantry.

I lower my voice to a whisper. "Did he say dildo?"

Axel can't quite hold in his laugh. "They sound the same. But it's dill dough, two words, dill as in pickle. Dough as in bread."

I get it now. "And they sell it? In their delis?"

"They have a bread of the month. It's in rotation.

They all have clever names. There's one called Frosty's Balls with macadamia nuts."

More boxes appear in the doorway until we're blocked in. Anthony peers over the top. "Don't do anything I wouldn't do in there."

One of the other men says, "It's Jason who does all the terrible deeds in the deli kitchen."

Then Sherman's voice. "What is Jason doing in the deli?"

Then another one says, "Focus, Dad, we're testing the proofing oven."

I open another box, discovering industrial-sized bottles of four kinds of mustard.

Axel opens another to find salt, pepper, and baking powder. "I bet they're going to need these in a minute."

We work companionably for a while, occasionally stopping to assess the space we have left against the contents of the boxes. We find a box of Tasty Pickle aprons and T-shirts.

Then more non-pantry items like register tape rolls and ballpoint pens.

We break down boxes and stack them against the shelves.

"Dare we peek out there and see what's happening?" he asks.

"Do we want to know?"

He grins down at me and the tense, sick feeling I had earlier dissolves away.

"I'll do the spying." He pauses in the doorway and bends slightly to look.

"What's happening?" I ask.

"They're all staring at the sink area."

"Is the faucet a Pickle deity?"

"That's funny."

Finally, Sherman says, "No, I think you're right, John Paul. The knife rack should go beside the sink, not over it."

"Is John Paul Havannah's dad?" I ask Axel.

He nods. "The two deli titans, going after each other."

"Finally, he sees reason!" John Paul booms.

I'm not sure I want to go out there. I busy myself by turning all the labels of the buckets of pickles to face outward.

But then the party comes to us.

"We need flour! Baking powder! Yeast!" John Paul is back, staring at us in the pantry.

I pass the items to Axel, who gives them to John Paul.

He turns to the kitchen. "Butter! Milk!"

"Pickles!" Sherman adds.

"No pickles!" John Paul shouts. "Peppers!"

"Pickles!"

"Peppers."

Havannah's tone conveys her frustration. "You can each make your own."

"Should we sneak out of here?" Axel asks.

"I'm not sure I can," I whisper. "It's my job."

Axel peers out of the pantry again. "I think if we jump the chopping block and dive through the opening to the seating area, we can make a run for it."

He always makes me laugh. "I'm not much for parkour."

"Right! Parkour. Just like in *The Office*." Axel shifts from side to side as if he's ready to take on the kitchen obstacle course.

"Yeah, and I'll be Andy, falling into a refrigerator box."

Axel holds up a finger to stop me. "No, it will be an *oven* box." He shouts, "Parkour!" And leaps into the kitchen and onto the butcher block.

Oh my God! He did it!

I step into the doorway to see.

Havannah grabs his leg. "We already put flour on the counter, you blockhead!"

"Parkour!" Axel yells, but he's brought down by the Pickle brothers, who haul him to the floor by the pants.

"Parkourrrrrr!" he continues yelling as he tries to escape.

Havannah shakes her head, wiping down the counter to spread flour again. The two elder men both punch balls of dough in stainless steel bowls.

Havannah spots me. "Calypso, maybe you and Axel can unwrap all the new tables and chairs. He needs to be kept out of trouble."

Axel pops up off the floor. "Aye, aye, captain!" He acts like he might dive through the serving window, but Havannah grabs him and turns him toward the door. Her flour-covered hands leave two prints on his shirt.

I step out to look around. Yonder and Joe are long gone. I'm the only non-family here. "Did you get all the produce put away?"

She nods. "But the fridges are too stuffed to organize. I could use someone to write down how much fits and keep inventory notes while we figure all this out. I'm used to a walk-in fridge."

"So is Jason," Anthony says, elbowing his brother.

"Shut up," Jason says.

"Nova says she got stuck to the permafrost in your freezer," Anthony says.

"Boys," Sherman warns, like they're all twelve.

I open the fridge, catching a bag of red peppers before it cascades to the floor. "Can we move the overflow to the main fridges of the big restaurant?"

"So smart," Havannah says. "Yes, please plan for that later, when the boys are gone."

"Okay." I shove the peppers back onto a shelf and quickly slam the fridge door.

Axel is already pulling plastic wrap off the furniture, so I leave the kitchen to join him. We start in the back corner, the farthest from the others.

"So what do you think of the whole Pickle crew?" Axel asks.

"They're… a lot."

"We are."

"I'm not sure I have them all sorted."

Axel tackles the wrap on a table. "Max, Jason, and Anthony are brothers. Their dad is Sherman. Their mom Patricia was my mom's sister."

"Was?"

"She died ten years ago. Mom was heartbroken. Aunt Pat was amazing."

"I'm sorry."

"We all were. My mom Caprice had my oldest brother Rhett, then Court, then me, then my baby sister Nadia."

"You guys have big families." I kneel to pull the plastic off a chair.

"Some do."

"Then Anthony married Magnolia, Havannah's sister."

"Right. And that's how John Paul and Sherman became rivals. There was some real bad blood for a while. Magnolia and Anthony had to fake an engagement to calm it down."

"But they're married?"

"Yeah. One thing you'll learn about the Pickle clan is that they don't do anything small or ordinary."

"And you?"

"I mean, I was naked on a mountain when I met you."

"And I had to use duct tape on my vijayjay."

"I love that word."

"I bet." I've never been one for sexy banter, but with Axel, it comes naturally.

We collect the plastic from the first table and chairs and stuff it into an empty box. Then we move to the next.

"I brought you more Laffy Taffy."

I let go of the chair I'm holding. "Where?"

He stands next to me, arms held out. "You have to find it."

"Axel!"

"You've seen me naked!"

"Axel!" I turn to look into the kitchen, but the Pickles are all staring into the new proofing oven. Apparently, the dough is inside.

I look him over before touching anything. Surely he wouldn't do anything as ridiculous as putting it near his crotch.

But I admit, looking at him in the casual hoodie and gray sweats is sweet in a different way from the tux. His shoulders are wide and strong. His thighs fill out the pantlegs.

And there's a bulge going on down there.

But the location of the Laffy Taffy is pretty obvious. I reach inside the front pocket of the hoodie, right over his belly. I encounter that hard slab of abs as I close my hands around the wrappers.

"Classic ones today," I say, recognizing the shape of the candy before I've even pulled it out.

"All for you."

I examine the bars in my palm. Two cherry. Two strawberry. "Perfection. Thank you."

"I have to do something to make sure you want to keep me around." His gaze holds mine, and my belly does that weird flip thing again.

We're staring at each other when Jason drums his hands on the stainless-steel prep counter. "Hey! Those tables aren't going to unwrap themselves!"

I step back, a cold, sick feeling slicing through me at the admonishment even though I know he's joking. He and Havannah are both grinning at us in a knowing way.

I shove the Laffy Taffy in my pocket and kneel by a chair to clear it off.

Axel gives his cousin the finger, then resumes tearing away the plastic.

It occurs to me we've done everything backwards.

See the private bits.

Meet the family.

And we haven't even gone on a date.

AXEL

As much as I want to spend all day with Calypso, I have to get back to my brothers. I don't see them all that often since they left Colorado, and based on the number of curse words texted to me in the last hour, they've awakened like bears.

So after all the plastic is off the furniture and I've said goodbye to my cousins, I drive back to Chez Axel on the mountainside.

Rhett sits at the table with a mug of coffee blacker than his soul and a bottle of ibuprofen. Court lies on the sofa, thumbing through his phone feed with one hand over an eye as if he needs to block the light.

"There are no random females wandering about, are there?" I ask, thumping Court's head.

He doesn't even move, like he's dead inside.

"Nah. They weren't the one-nighter type," Rhett says. He's looking ragged around the edges, his hair sticking up randomly, hunched over in his gray sweats.

Court sits up at that. "He means they turned him down flat."

"Heh." I sit next to Rhett at the table. "Losing your mojo?"

Court joins us, wincing at the scrape of the wood legs on the tile. "He tried to go for two, as it were. That didn't go over well."

Rhett throws a punch at Court, but he's slow, and Court dodges.

"What was it Jessica said? Oh yeah. 'This isn't Pornhub.'"

Rhett aims a finger at Court. "But she did know Pornhub."

I'm not impaired this morning, so when I threw a punch at Rhett, he's way too groggy to get out of the way. It lands on his unshaven cheek. "No wonder you're single."

Rhett bats my arm away. "Who was the lady in red you were dancing with? Last we checked, you were Tinderizing multiple marks."

"And calling them marks is another reason you're single."

"Shut up, pipsqueak." He leans over like he's going to put me in a headlock, but I easily shift aside and head to the coffeemaker. "Court, you need a cup?"

"Already had three."

I lift the empty carafe. "Should I make more?"

"Yes," they say simultaneously.

I empty the reusable filter, rinse it out, and refill it. When I make it back to the table, both of my brothers have their heads on their folded arms.

"Damn, you two. How much did you drink?"

Rhett holds up his hand, his thumb and forefinger an inch apart. "This much more than we should have."

"You didn't answer the question," Court says, his voice echoing in the cavern made by his arms and the tabletop. "Who was the chick?"

I can't tell them too much. The cactus burrs. Me hiking naked. They've always said my hobby would bite me in the ass. They assumed it would be a snake.

"She works at the castle."

Court's voice is still an echo. "Is that why you've been over there so much?"

"Maybe."

"She must be something if you are willing to wear tights for her."

For that, Court gets a smack on the arm. He doesn't flinch.

Rhett lifts his head. "I saw our cousins last night. They're all married off."

"Yep. Mom tells me about it every time I'm over there." I kick Rhett and Court under the table. "You need to see her. She expects you to stay in their house tonight."

Court sits up with a groan. "Ugh. We'd rather be here. She makes us eat healthy and there's no beer."

"We can borrow Axel's car and smuggle some in," Rhett says.

"She expects us all at dinner," I say. "So, you have six hours to pull your raggedy asses together."

Court stumbles back to the sofa. "I'm going to sleep. Wake me when it's time to buy beer."

Rhett heads to the coffeemaker to get another cup. "I'm ordering a pizza. You don't have a decent thing to eat here."

Obviously, he didn't find my taffy stash. "There's eggs. Cheese."

"I guess I could bite the corners off the cheese."

They are absolute Neanderthals.

He returns with coffee and the block of cheese. Before he can shove it in his mouth, I take it from him and place it on a combination cheeseboard and slicer.

I grab a loaf of whole grain bread I picked up at the farmer's market. It's not pre-sliced, so I snag a breadboard and a knife.

Rhett watches me do this with bleary eyes. "Dude, that's a lot of work for a cheese sandwich."

Court's head pops up from the sofa cushion. "Cheese sandwich? I'm starving."

"I'm still ordering pizza," Rhett says.

I slice the cheese and cut off a hunk of bread. I put it on a proper plate and slide it over to Rhett.

He picks it up in his meaty hands and takes a bite. His eyes flash as he looks at me. "Holy shit, this is good." He wolfs down half of it.

Court wanders back over. "I want some of that." He picks up the bread like he's going to rip a piece off.

I smack him with the flat edge of the knife. "Don't be an animal." I cut him bread and cheese as well.

He sinks his teeth in and collapses on the chair. "What is this God-like substance?"

I cut more. "Happy cows give better milk. Assembling food without filling it with chemicals makes it better."

Rhett waves me off. "We're just starving."

I aim the point of my knife at him. "You're a brute who deserves all the pesticides you get."

They down coffee, bread, and cheese like the Cookie Monster, with about the same amount of crumbs. My house is already a wreck, so I don't worry that much about it. I really should get help again. I prefer to hike and volunteer and dream up the next great nature app over scrubbing floors.

Dad thinks I should have a personal assistant and staff and all that, but for what? I don't do anything substantial. I have an accountant, and that seems to take care of the brunt of it.

Rhett seems more alive after some food. "You know, I expected you to build some crappy McMansion when you bought this land. And I thought it would really be up there." He waves his hand at the distant mountain peak through the floor-to-ceiling windows.

"I would have gone higher, but to avoid the mountains being overbuilt, Boulder won't issue water permits above a certain elevation." There are some things even half a billion dollars can't buy.

Rhett glances around. "It's cool, though. I saw the weight room. And the indoor to outdoor pool is killer."

Court looks up from his bread. "The hot tub is killer. In fact, I think I'll go get back in it."

"Drink some water first," I tell him. "You don't need to get any more dehydrated than you already are."

He stands up and waves me off. "Pipsqueak health nut." He takes off.

Rhett shakes his head. "Who knew you would be the crunchy granola one?"

I get comments like this all the time. It's fine. I eat pizza and drink beer like anybody else. I just choose well when I can.

I pick up their plates and leave them in the sink, grimacing at the pile. Okay, housekeeper, priority one on Monday.

Rhett brings his cup to the kitchen. "For what it's worth, I liked the girl. I mean, you didn't let us meet her. Wise choice, by the way. But you two looked good together. Happy."

"It's new," I tell him. "We'll see how it goes."

He claps me on the shoulder. "We won't tell Mom."

"Thanks." I'm not ready to be grilled about Calypso over dinner.

Rhett takes off for another part of the house, and I decide I better tackle these dishes. If there is even a slight possibility that Calypso could end up here this week, I don't want to risk looking like a slob.

And I do hope I can get her here.

18

CALYPSO

The deli is quiet after the Pickles leave. The cooking area is sparkling-clean, and several loaves of fresh bread sit on the cutting block, some plain, some with pickles, others with peppers.

The ovens have been adjusted and deemed in good working order. The knives and bowls and pots are all arranged, and the order of the deli line is marked with sticky notes for the first trial day.

Havannah asks me to reduce the overage in the fridges. She tells me to take any bread I want and give the rest to the main kitchen staff.

The silence is bliss after the roar of noise and the stress of too many people in a small space. I need the downtime.

I eat the bread for lunch. The pickle one is strange, but good. The sourdough is bliss. The pepper one is way too spicy, and I have to spit it out into the compost.

I carefully slice and wrap the rest of it and clean the counter. I drag a couple of empty boxes to the fridges and start pulling the overstock to move to the main kitchen.

I decide to create a veggie fridge and a dairy fridge. I organize the vegetables, creating neat stacks based on size and color for easy locating. Then, in the other, I make deep rows of butter, milk, cheese, eggs, and condiments.

I put some of the overstock back into the fridges once it's all neat. I'm down to one box when I proclaim the room ready to be closed up.

I take one more look in the pantry to see if it looks ready for use. The shelves are orderly. Some items have been shifted, no doubt by John Paul or Sherman while Axel and I unwrapped furniture. But it's fine. Some of this might make more sense to people who've worked in a professional kitchen. I certainly haven't.

I hear voices, and step out to see Havannah with a woman in a tall chef hat. She looks out of place in the small, casual kitchen.

"Calypso! You're still here." Havannah smiles at me. "We were admiring your fridge work."

"Thanks." I head to the box. "I was about to take this to the main kitchen."

"Oh, good." Havannah gestures to the woman. "This is Chef Monique. She's the kitchen manager for the restaurant. She'll be a resource for you as we move forward."

"Nice to meet you," I say.

"Looks like you have a good person right here to help get things started," Monique says. "Do you have any experience cooking?"

Havannah's gaze is on me, and I panic over what to say. "Not in a restaurant. But I cook at home."

"Can you chop?"

"Not in the perfect way I see on cooking shows."

She nods. "It's fine. Filo will train everyone. It will be a big part of the work in the deli. Can you bake?"

"I've made cakes. And normal things. Not much experience with bread."

"Yes, we don't make much bread in the restaurant. We will have to train on that as well." Monique opens the proofing ovens. "We don't even have these."

Havannah taps the top of the counter with her finger. "Calypso, do you have an interest in the kitchen, or does the idea horrify you?"

I'm not sure what to say. This is wildly different from my old career. But she doesn't know that. I didn't disclose my work history or my degree. "It was fun arranging things. I like bread."

She watches me a moment more. "How about we place you here while everyone gets oriented? You are incredibly smart and will be a great assistant manager even without the food experience. You have a knack for organization and maximizing space. I bet you will be quite adept right away at managing food orders and employee hours. Of course, we'll have an experienced manager to train and help you. How does that sound?"

Assistant manager? Wow. "Okay. I'm up for it."

"Excellent. Monique, when Filo arrives tomorrow, let's have a meeting with him and Calypso to go over the timeline for opening the deli and sorting through the employees to find the best fits." She turns to me. "Do you know where the conference room is?"

"I'm guessing the office wing, near where I interviewed?"

"Yes, two doors down from that." Havannah rubs her hands together. "This is great."

There's a "Mommy, Mommy!" from the hall, and a little boy runs into the kitchen, quickly followed by a tall man in jeans and a "King of the Castle" sweatshirt with the hotel logo.

Of course, he's the actual king of the castle, Havannah's husband, Donovan McDonald.

Havannah scoops the boy up. "Hey, baby. Fancy seeing you here."

"DonDon said you were making pickle bread." He squirms in her arms, trying to get down.

"We did. Grandpa John Paul was here."

"He makes pepper bread!"

"Well, so was Uncle Sherman."

I pull the wrapped extras out of the box I packed. "The bread is right here."

The boy isn't tall enough to see on the counter, so I lower a slice of wrapped pickle bread to show to him. "Is this the one?"

He looks up at me with shy eyes and glances at his mother.

"You can have it," she says.

He snatches it from my hands and takes off out the door. Donovan follows.

Havannah laughs. "I'll be right behind you."

I tuck the other bread back in the box.

"Thank you, Calypso. I'll see you in the morning. I don't think we'll need anything else from you today. I appreciate you getting here so early to install the oven. It was a great success."

I nod and pick up the box.

We file out of the kitchen and Havannah shuts everything down. I notice that she hangs by the door a moment, looking the deli over with a wistful expression. I understand she was brought up in her grandfather's deli, and only a few years ago opened one with her sister.

I'm guessing that since building the castle, she's missed those simpler days.

I know exactly how she feels.

My days feel complicated, too.

I drop off the box in the kitchen. Word has already gotten out that I will help manage the new deli, so the cooks and staff look at me differently. I'm not sure how I feel about that. I came here to hide.

But this is no big deal. It's still working deep in a castle, even further hidden in the small deli.

And at some point, I'll have to leave, anyway. I have an apartment in San Diego. Technically, I have a job at the engineering firm. I took personal unpaid leave, but I didn't resign. The timing was good, as the other engineer in my division had returned from maternity leave only a week before Jeremy's unexpected proposal.

And Jeremy. I don't owe him anything, not even my whereabouts.

But old habits die hard. Do what he says. Dress like he wants. Act like he expects.

I guess I did it and did it and did it, like I had for my parents before him, until I could do it no more.

And now, I can't even think about behaving in all the ways he required of me. For once, I'm completely, without reservations, unapologetically myself.

And Axel likes it. I wonder where he is, what he's doing. I have his number. I haven't used it yet.

The bed bounces as I flop on my belly. I pull the Laffy Taffy out of my pocket and unwrap the first one.

The joke reads, "How do you communicate with a fish? You drop it a line."

I guess that's a sign.

My finger glides over the screen to find Axel's number. I stare at it a good minute, gathering courage.

This shouldn't be so hard. I've kissed him, after all.

And I've seen him naked.

The thought of what I must have looked like sprawled on the trail with my panties on my ankle makes my face heat up. I can't even believe we're a thing after all that.

I type out the joke from the wrapper and add, "My taffy made me write you."

It's a minute of pure adrenaline before a text bubble appears.

> Axel: I love my candy even more.
>
> Me: Should I open one and see if we should run away together?

I stare at the words before I send them. It's so much

easier to flirt alone in my room with my phone. I shrug. Why not?

> Axel: Let me see if I can get in touch with the joke writers. What should it say to convince you?

My heart hammers at how he's flirting back. Is this for real? I feel like a teenager.

A flash of pure mischief flashes through me. I haven't acted this way since I was thirteen, before my junior prom, when I wanted to wear a *Sixteen Candles* replica dress and my mother had been horrified. I hadn't chosen my own clothes for anything important after that, not once. Graduation? Nope. Sorority rush? Hardly. First job interview? Not even that.

But I'm me now. Actual me.

> Me: Why did the chicken cross the road?
>
> Axel: Why?
>
> Me: To get to the cock.

I roll on my back. Did I really say that?

The dots appear and I wait with frenzied anticipation for what he might say. I would have never, ever written such a thing to Jeremy. He was hand-picked by my mother after meeting his mother at a charity event.

I had graduated college without finding a fiancé, which panicked her. She insisted all the "good ones" would be taken already.

The mothers arranged our first date, and it was pre-destined from the start. Jeremy wasn't cruel, not really, but he was definitely of the same mindset as the rest. To fit into the comfortable society where we belonged, we had to act a certain way. Join certain clubs. Do certain events.

Cock jokes wouldn't fly. Even when we moved to sleeping together, it was almost as if our mothers were watching. Like we couldn't do anything you couldn't show on network television.

I didn't love him, that's for sure. He became a routine, like brushing my teeth or ordering grocery delivery.

A text comes through. My heart hammers.

> Axel: I want an entire Laffy Taffy line with only your jokes.
>
> Me: I don't think I'm very funny normally.
>
> Axel: That can't be true. Every time I'm with you, I can't help but smile.

I roll over on my bed. This feeling is like being drunk. How did this happen? How long can it last?

> Axel: When can I see you again? I have family things tonight. But tomorrow? What are your work hours? When are you free? How can I be near you?

My head spins. Everything tells me this has to be some joke. I'm being pranked. I have to be.

After all my mother's efforts to make me look the part she wanted me to play, I never fit in anywhere

I couldn't make friends with the people I now looked

like, who also had designer outfits bought by a stylist and hair that cost more than a car payment. They might approach me, but the minute I talked, they realized I wasn't right. I didn't think the same way.

And I was regarded with mistrust by the free-thinkers I might have fallen in with if I could have been myself. I didn't look like them. I was a poser, an elitist. They didn't give me a chance.

It was a mess. There was this huge disconnect between the way I was forced to present myself and the way I felt inside.

I want an adolescent do-over. I want to go back to age thirteen and tell my mother to shove it. I will wear overalls and ring tees. I will paint art on my Converse and make every fingernail a different color. I'll use drugstore hair dye in every bright color.

I'll explore. Experiment. Figure out what's really me.

It isn't too late. I got away. This is my chance.

And I have Axel. This gorgeous, slightly oddball, naked-hiking man who can't get enough of me.

Also, he's probably sweating, waiting out my response.

My fingers fly on the phone keyboard.

> Me: I have a meeting with Havannah and the chefs tomorrow. They're making me the assistant manager of the deli. Not sure when I'll be off.

> Axel: Text me when you're out. I can help you in the deli. Havannah will let me. I'll be your own personal slave.

This makes me laugh. Strong, perfect Axel, doing my bidding?

Me: I'll let you know.

Axel: I can't wait.

Me: Me neither.

I stick the cherry taffy in my mouth and start Googling dirty jokes.

Tomorrow is the first day of the best part of my new life.

19

AXEL

Monday morning finds me rushing around my house, picking up random things. Socks. Beer cans. My brothers' pizza boxes. They ordered some before Mom's dinner, worried it would be too froufrou.

They were right. It was a Brussels sprout hash with balsamic-beet compote. I loved it. They sneaked out to eat leftover cold pizza from my car.

But upon hearing about my slovenly ways, Mom immediately called her housekeeping team and left a Sunday night message to please save her poor piggish son.

So they are coming. And I'm in shock at exactly how messy things are here. But also excited, because now Calypso can come.

If she wants.

Signs are favorable.

Mom suggested I not be there once they start, so I plan to head up to the hotel to help in the deli. I'm missing my hikes, of course, but to be honest, Calypso is a bigger high than the Rocky Mountain air.

I've thrown all my towels in the washing machine when the doorbell buzzes. I made it.

The team barely acknowledges me, having already gotten their instructions from Mom. There are four of them, three women and a man, and they make such quick work of the living room that I figure I better skedaddle or they'll be done before I start my car.

I hum along to the radio, tapping the steering wheel as I drive down the mountain to cross over to the highway that will take me to the castle. The pines are vivid green against the blue sky. The first snow will happen soon. Then it will be the holidays.

And I'll get to know Calypso more and more. Will she go home for Thanksgiving? Will we know each other well enough by then to take her to meet my parents? There's still two months. I'm ready to take her now. She's already met my cousins and Uncle Sherman.

I'm already planning snowy walks in matching knit hats when I realize I've blown right past the turn to the castle. Thankfully, there's a gas station a mile farther up, so I turn around there and head back.

But this splashes cold water on my thoughts. What am I doing? I barely know this woman.

The internal argument rages hot. But she wrote me! We click! And did you see that red dress? Remember that kiss?

I park in the employee spots near the donkey pens. The miniature donkeys are out, roaming their new digs. I look at them a moment, and one trots over. When I lift my hands to show that I don't have anything for them, it gives a phbbbllltttt sound and trots off again.

"Right back at ya!" I yell.

I'm in a jolly, indefatigable mood when I open the back door and enter the storeroom. It's bustling, as usual, this time with bulk deliveries of Kleenex and toilet paper.

I wave to Yonder, who's watching the boxes. "Is Calypso in the deli?"

He nods. "She's going to be helping manage it. I hate to lose her on my team, but they nabbed her!"

"Great!" I already knew that, but I can't let on. Calypso has to take the lead on letting anyone know that we're an item.

And we are, I think. She messaged me a cock joke. That doesn't sound friend-zoned.

I head through the maze and spot the back door to the deli kitchen propped open with a box. When I head in, Calypso is there alone. I'm tempted to put my arms around her, but I have to check myself.

Our tight future is all in my head. In reality, we haven't been on a date. I've only danced with her and walked the castle. There was the one kiss, but that might have been us caught up in a moment. I have no real right to sneak-attack her with another.

All this has gone through my head in the ten steps from the door to the fridge where she's peering in. But when she closes the door and straightens, her pixie hair curling around her face, her eyes happy to see me, all that goes straight out the window.

I draw her close and press my lips to hers.

She relaxes against me, and I kiss her more. I feel like I'm drowning. The one evening apart feels like a year.

She pulls back, grinning, but pokes my chest. "We're going to get caught, you crazy man."

"I couldn't help myself."

She holds up a little glass dish with a pickle relish in it. "What's this?"

"Looks like Grammy Alma's sweet pickle relish."

Her eyes light up. "Ooooh. I love sweet pickle relish."

"We should eat it then!" I open the drawer that John Paul and Uncle Sherman had argued over, that now contains the utensils. I snag a spoon.

"Should we eat it right out of here?" she asks.

"There isn't much there. They were probably testing. I say we get a taste and then toss it. The staff will make more." I pull the saran wrap off the top.

She peers in. "I'll probably be totally done with pickles after working here a while."

I nod. "You might." I dip the spoon in. "Ready for a taste of heaven?"

She quirks a smile. "That wasn't your kiss?"

"Second best in heaven."

She opens her mouth, and I'm reminded of our Laffy Taffy moment. Everything is so easy with Calypso. I've never met anyone I meshed with so well, so fast.

I spoon a decent-sized bite in her mouth, then kiss her so we can share the taste of it.

Sexy. When we part, we grin at each other over our

mouthfuls, then her expression changes. A split second later, mine does, too.

Oh, no. This isn't sweet relish. Or even Anthony's love relish he made when he and Magnolia were on a TV tour.

It's the ghost pepper relish.

I dash to the sink and spit the relish into the disposal. Calypso quickly follows suit. She blasts the water on and sticks her face in it, running the water over her mouth.

I dance in small circles. I've had the ghost pepper recipe before, but only in a small dose. I guess they made this while Calypso and I were unwrapping tables.

Finally, she backs away, and I dive for the faucet. Milk is better, but we're in a hurry. I use the sprayer to wash out my mouth, still feeling bits of fiery ghost pepper lingering between my teeth.

"Even my lips burn!" Calypso cries, pressing her fist to her mouth.

I turn long enough to say, "First aid kit!"

She hurries to the pantry, emerging with the sealed red plastic box.

I leave the sink, feeling less like my face is on fire, and help her open the box.

We dump the contents onto the counter. I spot the packets of medicated lip ointment, which Uncle Sherman added to the kits precisely for this emergency. I tear one open and smear it over her lips, then mine.

Finally, she relaxes against the counter. "Holy shit, Axel. That was a kiss of death."

I laugh. "It was."

Then she laughs, and I laugh harder, and soon we're

busting a gut, trying to put away the kit, bent over. I put the kit back in the pantry while she washes out the sink.

When we're back at the chopping block, she says, "I'm not sure I can risk kissing you again after that."

"Oh yes, you will."

"You're sure you can convince me?"

"Positive."

"All right, Mr. Sure-of-Himself. We'll continue that when I'm off the clock. Without the fire relish."

Will we?

"When's that? Please say one hour, two tops. That's all I can wait."

She bites back a smile. "You're crazy. You don't even know my full name."

She turns to an iPad sitting on the counter and touches the screen, bringing up a long list of type.

I lean against the edge of the stainless steel sink to watch her. It looks like she's taking inventory.

"Let me guess."

She glances at me a second, then types in a few more numbers. "Do you even know my last name?"

"Ash. Calypso Ash."

"All right. So go for the middle."

"Lynn. Ann. Lee."

"That's low-hanging fruit, but no." She opens the fridge again.

"Emily. Elizabeth. Grey."

"Nope." She peers into the shelves.

"Christina, Lindsey, Laura."

"Do you realize how many names are in the world?" She closes the fridge and taps on the iPad again.

"I'm happy to say them all if it means I get to stay in here with you."

She darts her eyes at me again, but I see the way they shine. "Keep it going, then."

"Amelia, Hannah, Amber."

"Are you going to remember which ones you've already said?"

"No."

She types in a few more numbers, then turns to me. "I'll narrow it down for you. My initials are a government agency."

I think for a minute while she returns to the fridge. "IRS. DEA."

She peers over the door, laughing. "My first name is Calypso!"

"Right. Right. CBS."

"That's a TV station!" She's laughing so hard that the door swings closed.

"Give me a minute." I hold up a finger. "I never said I was a genius."

"Think about the FBI," she says.

"That doesn't start with C."

She's giggling, a melodious sound that makes my whole body warm over.

"I was trying to make you think of the other super common agency. FBI and…" She holds out her arms like she's prompting me to come up with the other.

And I have it. "CIA."

"Ding, ding, ding! Finally!" She manages to control her laughter. "But I'll admit, my middle name is unusual."

"Yeah, 'I' names aren't common." I hop onto the chopping block. "Ivy. Iris. Iodine."

She starts laughing again, and her finger misses the iPad screen. "Iodine?"

"Maybe your parents are science geeks!"

"And *Axel*, yours are what, automotive repair geeks?"

"Wagon wheels, thank you very much for poking my hurt." I manage a pout.

She gets serious a minute, so I change my expression. "Kidding. I'm named for the singer in the 80s hair band."

"Guns 'n Roses?"

"That would be it."

"You don't have an e in your name?"

I sigh. The story of my life. "I do. They didn't know how he spelled it."

"Oh. Gosh." The giggles hit her again. "I'd stick with the wagon wheel story."

"Okay. Moving on. Imogene. Isabelle. Ichabod."

"Ichabod?" She rests her arm on the edge of the counter, pressing her head onto it, her shoulders shaking. "My stomach hurts from laughing. Please… stop."

"Invinia."

She straightens suddenly. "That's it!"

"Really?"

"Yes! How did you guess it?"

I shrug my shoulders. "I don't know. It just came to me!"

"Did you know it all along?" Her stare pins me, but I can see the smile flirting with her mouth.

"I didn't!"

"Well, that's wild. So, what's yours?"

Oh, we went there. "I already told you."

She shakes her head. "No, you didn't."

"I sort of did." I try to be good-humored about this topic, but it wasn't easy in the cutthroat years of middle school.

"You said you were named for Axl Rose."

I can tell when the light dawns. Her eyes widen. "Uh oh. They didn't."

I sigh. "They did."

"You don't have any sisters they could have foisted that middle name on?"

"I was supposed to be the last. I ended up with a baby sister years later, though."

"And her name is?"

"Nadia Marie."

"But Nadia Rose would have been so pretty."

"Could have been. But she was an unplanned surprise. So I got the rose."

"Axel Rose Armstrong. It is a nice delicate center to your very manly first and last."

"I can handle it. At least now that I'm not twelve."

She fires up the iPad. "I have to inventory the pantry. Come in here with me, and I'll kiss you and make it all better."

She doesn't have to ask me twice.

The moment we're inside, she sets the iPad on a shelf and turns to me, grabbing both sides of my face. "This is for all the mean people who made fun of your beautiful floral name." She stands on tiptoe to kiss me.

I wrap my arms around her and draw her close. I've

never had a relationship go like this. There's usually the ask. The date. A jump or two into the sack. A slow disintegration as we realize the only thing we had in common was rock climbing or ultimate frisbee or a brand of running shoe. Then the slow ghosting into nothing.

But not this.

Calypso is like cliff diving at night. It's a freefall into the unknown, having to blindly trust that it's going to be the ride of your life and not an obliterating crash.

Our mouths are hot and greedy. I kiss her jawline, moving down. But she wears a hotel hoodie and I can't get anywhere.

I groan in frustration. "We're not dressed for this."

She drops her forehead to my shoulder. "And it's a good thing. I probably should avoid getting fired on my first day as assistant manager of the deli. I kind of need this job."

I hold my breath, wondering if she'll say anything about her degree or her life before coming here, but she lets go of me.

I step back. She's right. I'm not sure why she's here or what she's running from, but I shouldn't put her position in peril. Not that Havannah would overreact. She has a history of her own that makes her give people the benefit of the doubt.

But it's unlikely her employees know that. I'm privy to her past due to family.

"So, inventory." I scoop up the fallen boxes to put them back on the shelves. "Looks like five containers of dried cranberries, twenty ounces each."

Calypso straightens her hoodie and pickles up the

iPad. "Got it. Next, how many ten-pound bags of flour?"

I'm perfectly content to work in this pantry with her. Anywhere she is, mountainside or deli, I'm happy to be, too.

20

CALYPSO

The new deli manager is Filo, a mid-fifties man from the room service group. He has a wife and three teenaged kids. The oldest works as a bellboy.

He's waiting in the deli kitchen when I arrive Tuesday morning. He's already decked in the green Tasty Pickle cap and apron. His ample belly brushes against the chopping block as he expertly dices an onion. His mouth twists to one side, making his tiny mustache lopsided. He reminds me of Boris from the old *Rocky and Bullwinkle* cartoon.

I stand and wait until he gets to the end of the onion, marveling at how cleanly he sweeps all the pieces into a bin hanging off the end of the counter.

"You must be Calypso," he says, lifting the clear container from the hooks to consider how full it is. "Are you ready to learn to chop?"

"I guess so."

He slides the onion bin back into place and takes in my jeans and gray sweatshirt. "This outfit will never do.

Go into the pantry and put on short sleeves. Long sleeves will get in the way and end up messy. Also, the apron and hat. We may not be serving customers yet, but we must get used to looking like the great purveyors of the Tasty Pickle!"

He lifts his arm in the air at the end, light glinting off the blade of the broad knife. In any other scenario, I might have been terrified. But if this were the analogy portion of the SAT, I would say that Filo is to cooking as Axel is to hiking.

They both get pretty passionate about their pursuits.

I close myself in the pantry and pluck a small green T-shirt off the stack I organized yesterday. I whip off the sweatshirt and replace it. When the sweatshirt is tucked away, I tie on the apron and stick the round, flat-topped fabric hat on my head.

If my parents could see me in this getup, they'd wail and gnash their teeth. I'm a long way from the San Diego Country Club.

Thank goodness.

When I emerge from the pantry, Axel has arrived. "It's chopping day!" he says.

"You're here early." Yesterday, he rolled in closer to noon.

"It's raining. No hike today."

Filo nods. "Cats and dogs. Took me half an hour to get here. Everybody drives so slow!"

This is the fourth weekday Axel's been able to come over. I wonder what he does for work. I don't have any social media installed on my phone whatsoever, so I haven't tried finding him online. I suppose I could Google him and see if anything turns up.

Or I could ask.

So I do.

"Are you on vacation? Or do you work nights? Or work at all?"

He hesitates, and I wonder if he does something seedy, like host an OnlyFans of his feet. Or if he's a stripper. He could totally be a stripper.

But it's Filo who speaks up. "Axel here wrote a killer nature app. It's super great. It tells you where to hike and keeps you from getting lost."

"Oh! So you're an app developer?"

He nods. "Working on the next thing now."

He must set his own schedule. I like it.

Filo's gray eyebrows knit together. "Why is the big hiking man here to chop onions?"

"I can hang with anybody. Maybe I'll write the next great cooking app instead."

Filo grins. "I love it. And I will teach you it all!"

Axel breaks out in a smile. "Perfect."

"Look the part," Filo says. "Get on your uniform so you can be a Tasty Pickle inside and out."

Axel turns to me, his head tilted, and as soon as our eyes meet, we burst into an outrageous case of laughter.

Filo's eyebrows do their thing, running his last line through his head. Then he gets it and rolls another onion to the center of the block, a smile flirting with his mouth.

"Come on," I gasp out. "I'll get you a shirt." I grab Axel's sleeve and lead him to the pantry.

But once we're through the door and out of sight of Filo, his lips are on mine. His hands grasp the back of my neck and press me to him, the warmth of his mouth already one of my favorite things.

I lose my head a minute, the ground swooping out from under me. The laughter, the kiss, the unexpectedness of it all. I've never led a life like this. I didn't think it was possible.

Filo's voice booms from the other room. "You've gotten too quiet in there!"

We break apart in another burst of laughter. "I finally found a shirt that should fit you!" I say too loudly, passing one to Axel.

I step back as he pulls his long-sleeve tee over his head.

Then I'm not laughing. The sight of him makes my whole body tingle. His muscles ripple and shift. A trail of light hair low on his belly disappears into his jeans.

He catches me looking and leans in so close that his bare chest brushes my arm. "One day, we're going to do unspeakable things in this pantry," he whispers.

He steps back to whip on the shirt, and I'm still quivering. Then he's grabbing a hat and an apron, and his friendly face is ready for Filo. "I'm all set and very tasty."

That's for sure. I straighten my hat and follow him out. Filo has three onions and three knives set out on the block.

"All right, you two. The first rule of chopping is to create a stable surface to cut. So, if your object is round, you must create a flat side." He cuts off a slice, then turns the onion so it is resting solidly on the block.

I pick up my knife to cut the onion, but Filo shouts, "No, no, no!"

I jerk the knife away. "What?"

"The tip of the knife does not leave the table. And your fingers, they are all ready to be chopped!"

I glance at Axel, who shrugs.

Filo shifts my fingers on the onion so they are curled and out of the way. Then he places the knife in my hand, pressing the tip on the block and demonstrating how to rock the knife down.

I make the slice.

"Good, good." He turns to Axel. "Now you."

Axel tries to arrange his hands properly, but he must press too hard, because suddenly, the onion zips across the table and rolls off the edge.

Filo sighs. "It is only day one. It is fine. Wash the onion. We will go again."

Axel grins at me as he fetches the errant onion and takes it to the sink.

I think maybe we're both in over our heads.

Axel returns and plops his wet onion on the counter.

Filo blows out a long gust of air. "Pat it dry, please. We do not need the extra moisture in the onion bin."

Axel nods and picks up a dish towel from the stack. He rolls the onion inside it.

I send him a commiserating glance.

"Try again," Filo booms. "And put your concentration on it!"

Axel grabs the onion firmly and angles the point of

his knife at the block. As he brings it down with swift force, Filo yells, "Watch your—"

But he is way too late. The onion slice comes neatly away, but a line of red wells up on the tip of Axel's middle finger. Then pink spreads across the block.

"Don't bleed on the food!" Filo says. He snatches up the towel and presses it into Axel's hand. "Back up!"

Axel holds the towel, and my heart speeds up at how fast it blooms red.

"Let me see the cut," I say. "You may need stitches."

"I'm fine," he insists.

"Come over to the sink." I push him across the room and remove the towel.

As expected, I can't see anything for the blood, so I turn on the water. "It might sting," I say.

"Can't be worse than your cactus needles."

He has me there.

I rinse his finger and lift his hand to my nose so I can peer at it. There's a good cut, but it's not deep. "You'll live," I tell him. "I'll get the first aid kit."

Filo leans on the chopping block while I fetch an antiseptic spray and a stretchy Band-Aid designed for fingers.

Axel watches me while I tend to him. "It's like *Beauty and the Beast.*"

"I'm no beauty, and you're not a beast." I let go of his hand.

"I beg to differ on both counts."

"Then I'm looking forward to seeing the beast." That happy flirty feeling comes over me, the one I never got to use in my old life. I had the same problem dating as making friends. I looked like I should hook up with the popular boys with their trendy clothes and nice cars. But the boys I was interested in were the quirky ones. The science nerds. The art students. The ones whose primary sport was ping pong in the garage.

But now there's Axel. He's both quirky *and* a catch.

The wrappers stick to the damp counter, but I peel them off and drop them in the trash. When I turn around, Filo is handing a bleach spray bottle and a paper towel to Axel. "For your blood."

I reach for them. "I'll do it."

Filo pulls them back. "This is how you learn. You make a mess. You clean it up."

"He's *injured*."

Axel takes the bottle and towel. "I'm fine."

Filo watches me, and I stare at him right back. I've done enough capitulating to my family for a lifetime. I won't do it to this man. "So, if he chopped his hand off, you would make him clean up the blood while we waited on an ambulance?"

"You exaggerate to no good point," Filo says. "It's all brain science. If you take some time to manage the consequences of a mistake, your brain will associate the mistake with bad things and teach your muscles not to do it again."

"I think his brain gets it after bleeding all over the onion."

"It is not enough in this case. The whole hand? I agree. But not that tiny slice. You will see the same attitude with the ovens. Early burns prevent later catastrophes."

"It's barbaric," I say.

"It is safety," Filo insists. "A minor mistake now means no big injury later. I have been doing this for a long time. You must trust me."

I don't. But Axel cleans up the blood and sanitizes the surface, then washes it down so there will be no bleach on the food. The pink-tinged onion goes into compost.

Filo sets another one on the counter, and we resume.

"This time, curl your fingers," Filo says. "Get them out of the way. One careful slice. Do not go after it like a machete in the jungle."

Axel nods. When we have successfully flattened our onions, the lesson moves on to slicing and dicing.

Whenever Filo turns away, Axel and I mimic his expressions and gestures, dissolving into laughter only to straighten up when he turns back to us.

This feels good. Filo is the middle school teacher, and Axel and I are the naughty young students.

I really am getting my do-over.

And I have the best accomplice.

21

AXEL

It turns out I'm useless in a kitchen.

I always thought I had a decent set of skills for a dude raised by a mom who did everything. I make the occasional meal kit and toss inventive salads full of nuts and seeds. I've pan fried a steak multiple times, and I can make pasta and mix it with a pre-made sauce like a boss.

But on Tuesday, when I pull my first pillow of dough out of the proofing oven to see if it has risen properly, Filo throws up his hands like I've cursed in front of my kindergarten teacher. "What have you done?"

Calypso bites her lip as she sets her metal bowl on the block. Her dough is perfectly rounded and pale, a smattering of flour across the surface.

I plunk mine down next to it. It looks like someone puked banana pudding.

Filo peers at Calypso's. "Very nice. Round. Good elasticity. Perfect shape. You are ready to bake."

He turns to me. "What did you do to it? A witch's curse?"

"I made it like you said."

"Is there yeast?"

"Yes, I measured it out."

"Did you use warm water?"

"Yes, it almost scalded my hand!"

Calypso turns at that, her mouth in the shape of an "o."

Uh, oh.

Filo's face goes scarlet. "Scalded! Did I say hot water? Did I say water so hot that it will burn?"

"No."

"What did I say, Axel Armstrong, nature hiker?"

"Warm water."

"Warm activates the yeast!" Filo's fingers swirl in the air, like he's making magic. "Hot water kills it!"

"So I killed the yeast."

"You killed the yeast!"

"Can I put more in there?"

"It has already been proofed!" Filo picks up the hot bowl with a dish towel and dumps the dough in the compost. "Again!"

Okay. I'll do it again.

"Calypso," Filo says, "You may move on to the wheat bread. I am going to check on my other crew." He heads out the door, still gesturing like he's continuing his lecture to me.

Calypso and I wait until he's gone, then burst out laughing.

She lifts her finger in the air. "You killed the yeast, you murderer! And the dough perished."

"I am a cereal killer!" I dunk my hands in the flour and dash around the counter, aiming for her.

She shrieks and takes off, racing out of the kitchen and into the dining room.

"You cannot run from the man who kills the yeast!" I trap her in the corner and she doubles over with laughter when I smack her ass with the flour, leaving huge white handprints on the back of her apron.

She looks down. "You're leaving your mark on me!"

"I'll do more than that!" I press her into the corner, my mouth on hers. She relaxes immediately, melting against my body. She tastes of the pinches of dough we ate to make sure they weren't too salty. She's like the perfect meal, warm and smelling of fresh bread and homemade dinners.

I want to devour her. I deepen the kiss, my hands on her back. I want to know her body better, touch more of her. But she gets unsure in these moments, as if she can't quite let go. So I keep it light and flirty and easy.

Voices filter in from the hall, and we break apart even though only employees with the right credentials can be keyed into the deli.

When the people pass by, we laugh like we're busted teenagers. I take in her flour-dusted body. "There's a lot of evidence of what we were up to."

She looks down. "Axel!" She shakes out the apron to clear the flour.

"Come on. Show me how you made your perfect

bread." I take her hand and lead her back to the kitchen. "We don't want mean old Mr. Filo to catch us."

By the time he returns, I'm halfway through kneading a second round and Calypso is working on the wheat. Filo nods in approval. "Tomorrow, we will bring in potential employees to learn. Make sure you have command of the process so that you look competent before your staff."

Calypso's face goes serious. "I will."

"And what of your boy?"

I shrug. "I'm the comic relief. I make everyone else look good."

Filo stares at me for long moments before saying, "I can see the value of that. Just don't bleed in my kitchen!" He peers through the window of the oven. "Calypso, when you have finished your loaves, we should meet in my office for administrative duties. We will need to consider the opening week orders and make projections. We will have to adjust considerably for a great while before we have a good system."

"Will do, Filo."

He heads for the door. "And do not do anything unsanitary on the kitchen block. Or if you do, make sure you bleach it all."

Then he's gone.

Calypso busts out in a laugh. "He's on to us."

I punch the dough one more time, then hop onto the counter, settling my butt in the flour. "Come here. Let's be unsanitary."

She moves between my knees, and we resume the kisses, tasting each other. Tomorrow, when the others arrive, we will stop having time alone. I can only hope she'll be ready for time outside the castle. If not my house, then at least a restaurant, or a walk in Boulder.

I want to spend every moment I can with her. I haven't laughed this much in a long time, and I'm pretty sure she hasn't either.

22

CALYPSO

Axel helps out for the next few days as we bring in potential deli workers from the new staffing pool to see who likes the work. He's funny and self-deprecating, which alleviates the frustration of those who utterly fail at chopping or bread making.

We make out in the pantry once everyone's gone, but no matter how pent-up I feel, I don't invite him to my room. Not yet. Something about my time with him feels isolated and temporary.

I'm not sure if it's the castle or just me knowing about my problems back home. But I can't see a future with Axel. I can't see my future at all.

When I get my first paycheck, I'm not sure what to do with it. I opted for paper checks to avoid giving away my California bank. I haven't opened an account here.

I'm paralyzed with fear that my parents or Jeremy will hire someone to find me. It won't be hard now. I have a new employer and tax records pointing to me being here. It couldn't be helped.

My old life will need addressing eventually. My bills are automatically paid for rent, utilities, and the phone still sitting in my apartment in San Diego. But my bank account isn't endless. I have three, maybe four months before I have to deposit more money or I will overdraft.

The assistant manager wage isn't anything close to my engineering salary. It won't be enough to cover me for long. My California rent is obscene.

My days are numbered before I have to make hard decisions. And I want to make them without the pressure of my family. These last two weeks have been the first time I have felt like I could breathe since I was a kid.

Since the deli isn't open yet, I get an actual weekend off, something that won't happen much once we have real hours.

Axel arrives with lunch on Saturday, and we walk out to the rose court, a central breezeway between two wings of the castle. It's chilly out, but that means we are alone.

I tighten my light jacket around me. I'll need something warmer soon. Colorado is a far cry from the temperature in San Diego.

He's brought hot soup, and the steam feels amazing on my face as we huddle close together at a table, protected from the wind by two trellises covered in empty rose vines.

We grin at each other as we skip the spoons and drink the soup straight from the waxy paper cups. Axel knows all the local farm-sourced restaurants.

"This week has gone by fast," I tell him. "You made

it so much fun. I think Filo might have run me off otherwise."

"Oh, he's a big teddy bear."

"A bear with a chef's knife!"

"He's been here since the castle opened. Havannah trusts him."

"He'll be run ragged when the deli is operational if she leaves him managing room service as well as the deli."

"I have a feeling she's prepping you for that job."

I set down my cup. "Really?"

He watches my face. "You don't want it?"

I'm not sure what to say without sounding ungrateful. "I never saw myself as a deli manager."

"Do you hate it?"

"We haven't opened yet. It's been like cooking camp so far."

He nods. "Do you have other dreams?"

I have no idea what to say to that. I could tell him I'm an engineer. That my last project was on a team charged with redesigning a complex intersection so that traffic would flow more freely.

But maybe managing a deli line isn't that much different. It's all about maximizing space and timing. I'll be moving sandwiches instead of cars. And I shouldn't pretend I was some great engineer. I was on a team and mostly I had to type the notes and check the calculations for mistakes. It takes decades to be in charge of anything important.

Here, I'd be the big cheese.

Literally.

I decide to turn the question around. "Do you have dreams? What's your next big project?"

He shrugs. "The hiking app was a fluke. I saw a brilliant design and adapted it for nature walks. I didn't think it was that revolutionary."

"I bet other people don't think so. Can I see how it works?"

"Sure." He pulls out his phone and swipes to the small square with the silhouette of a person on a mountain.

The image moves to a background of trees swaying against a blue sky. Two rectangles slide elegantly into view. One says, "Find a trail nearby." The other says, "Plan a future hike."

"It's pretty." I press "Find a trail nearby."

A map spins into position, and we become a pulsing red dot. I panic for a minute, recognizing the location services function, then remember this is his phone, not mine. I haven't revealed anything about myself to the Internet.

A series of circles pop up, each with a number value on them.

"What do these mean?"

"It's the difficulty level of the hike. Under fifty is easy. Over two hundred is strenuous."

There's a big variety in the mountains near the castle. I click on one that is ranked 150. A series of data fills the top half of the screen, and the bottom half is a video showing the vistas of the trail.

"That's nice." I pass him the phone. "Is it an ongoing project?"

"No, I sold it."

"Oh. So you've moved on."

He nods. "I have. And you?"

"I guess my big dream at the moment is eating a spicy relish without dying."

His mouth in a smile is something to behold. I never get tired of looking at it. "You'll have to look up the footage from when my cousin Anthony was on a cooking show and accidentally fried the mouth of the host with a ghost pepper pickle."

"Oh, no!"

"Oh, yeah. It was a huge deal."

"I might remember something about that."

"It was all over the internet." He takes my hand in his. "I'm glad you're here."

I'm relieved he has let me off the hook about my future. "Me, too. It's supposed to be warmer tomorrow. Shall we go on a hike? I saw some pretty low numbers on that map. And you could point out any cacti. You know, help out my girl parts."

"I would like very much to help out your girl parts." His voice has a low rumble to it. "And I'd be thrilled to take you on a hike."

"With clothes on," I add.

"Spoilsport."

I punch his arm. "Maybe someday."

"Mmmm," he says. "I will hold you to that."

I lean my head on his shoulder. I'm going outside my

comfort zone. But Axel's done it all week, and has the finger scar to prove it.

I can shift a little in his direction.

And maybe soon, I'll be able to tell him more about where I'm at.

And hopefully, figure out where I'm going.

23

———

AXEL

I enjoy hiking all ways. Alone. With a friend. With a group.

I've taken women on trails before. Normally they are pretty advanced, because I meet them in the context of a group or class or skill development.

But when Calypso and I leave my Land Rover behind at the end of a dirt road and set off on an easy trail on the upper ridge of my property, I feel damn near elated.

I've chosen this path for its ease, its beauty, and some interesting structures that have been left behind from other eras. It's the reason I bought this parcel.

It's also private. Mine. And this is the first time we're fully alone. I'm prepared for anything, or nothing, whatever she wants.

"That's a mighty big bag you have there," she says as I sling the backpack over my shoulders.

It's because I have everything I could use for an

overnight, should the need arise. A tent, bedrolls, food, water.

Condoms.

But I don't tell her that.

"I brought a picnic."

"You must eat like a bear." Her eyes go wide. "Will there be bears?"

I chuckle. "No bears."

"And mountain lions only at night."

"Right."

"And the evil squirrels had a name. You said it that first time."

"Chickarees. They will protect their tree nests."

"Right, chickarees." She raises a fist to the mountain. "I will avenge my girl parts!"

"We will take on the chickarees together."

She considers my pack. "I'm not carrying anything. That doesn't seem fair."

"I'm experienced. Unless you do a lot of long walks, you might start feeling the strain before long."

"Axel Rose Armstrong, are you saying I'm out of shape?"

"No!" Except, I don't think she's done much since I met her.

"I'll have you know I did ten sit-ups this morning!"

I try to control the smile taking over my mouth.

"I mean, it's because there was some gnat flying around my head when I was trying to sleep in, but I launched straight up off the pillow at least ten times trying to swat it!"

I let the laugh free. "Then you did ten more sit-ups than me."

"Ha. I out-exercised the master." She one-two punches my belly. "I'm going to have abs of steel like you by tomorrow."

I grab one of her hands and spin her in a dance circle. "Come on, you wild and crazy thing. Let's hit the trail."

She puts her foot up on a rock. "We shall conquer Mount…" She turns to me. "Mount what?"

"Green Mountain."

"We shall conquer Green Mountain today!"

"All right, Reinhold, let's get cracking." I head for the slender line of shoal that marks the trail.

She falls in behind me. "Who's Reinhold?"

"Reinhold Messner. He was the first person to climb all seven summits."

"What are the seven summits?"

"Kilimanjaro, Elbrus, McKinley, Aconcagua, Massif, Puncak Jaya, Everest."

"You sure can rattle those off." Calypso is already breathing a little heavy, so I slow my steps. I forget that I tend to go at a punishing pace.

"Hiking is my thing."

"Have you climbed any of those peaks?"

"No. There is a difference between a hiker and a mountain climber. I like the journey. I want to pause, study things. The summit isn't the point."

"Huh. I like that."

I grin back at her. Her cheeks are flushed a pale pink and her short brown hair flies around her head. She looks adorable in her green sweatshirt and yoga pants. She's in tennis shoes, though. I'll have to look for an excuse to gift her hiking boots.

But today's hike has no trouble spots and no need for specialized shoes or equipment. Every once in a while we have to climb a short rise of rock, and I turn to hold her hand as we go up.

It's only half an hour before we reach the first thing I want to show her. It's the ruins of a mountain cabin, probably built in the eighteen hundreds. Only a stone floor and the rock chimney remain, but it's a great place to take a break.

"Someone lived here?" Calypso asks as I set down the pack and pour us water.

"Probably not full-time. Hunters would build small structures to protect them from the elements each season."

Calypso takes her water and walks along the stone surface, running her hands over the chimney stones. "Wild how these have stood the test of time."

I watch her over the rim of my cup. She spots a cactus by the corner of the cabin and kneels down to inspect it.

She takes her time, gently touching the flat paddles covered in long needles.

"Playing with fire?" I ask.

"Maybe. I don't see what got me."

I squat next to her. "The barbed glochids are at the base of the long needles on this variety." I point to them. "But you would have felt the needles before getting to the glochids. I bet you encountered the type that relies solely on glochids for protection."

She sits back. "How did you learn all this?"

"I was a curious kid. I was always running off after wildlife or gathering plants."

"Did you grow up here?"

"New York, actually, but not Manhattan. Upstate."

"How did you end up in Boulder?"

"My parents moved here my senior year, and I stayed for college."

"To study app development?"

"Sort of. I had four majors."

"Did you get four degrees?"

Ah, this old problem. She hasn't Googled me. But at least all the articles about my life leading up to the monumental app keep me honest. "I didn't graduate with any of them."

"Oh." She sips her water. "Did something happen?"

"I wasn't a very good student. I sort of flunked out of all four departments."

"Oh."

"Does this upset you?"

She meets my gaze. "No! No. It's just a surprise. I don't meet many people who take such a hard run at college and don't make it."

"I'm doing all right."

"I bet."

"Is this changing your mind about me?" An uneasy feeling uncurls in my gut.

"I think it's great you figured out what you were good at without a piece of paper saying so."

Does she mean it? She isn't looking away. "What about you?" I ask, knowing I'm treading on troubled territory. "Did you go to college?"

"Oh. Right. Yes." She downs her water and passes me the cup. "I did. And then I ended up here! Managing a deli." She laughs. "Are we going to keep going?"

Deflection. I'm disappointed that she isn't sharing more, especially after I had to confess my failure. But I didn't mention my success either, at least not more than Filo already told her.

I'm going to, though. It's part of my plan for this hike. Maybe then she'll tell me more.

We head up a slightly steeper incline, and I keep watch to make sure Calypso is doing well. But she's cheery and has no trouble. When she spots our next destination, she sucks in a breath. "This is on your property?"

"It is. It's one of only a few standing fire towers left in Colorado."

She peers at it, shielding her eyes from the sun. "I would have thought those would be on federal or state property."

"This is a private one. It was built in 1902. The top structure fell off in the sixties, but the rest is intact. The walkway is structurally sound. Are you afraid of heights?"

"I've been to the Empire State Building and the Eiffel Tower without incident."

This tells me a fair amount about her upbringing. "Those are good heights. I like all kinds of summits, and traveling is how you get perspective. Let me know if you feel uncomfortable."

We approach the concrete base of the fire tower. This part alone is taller than us, with a steel door edged in crumbling rubber.

"Is there anything inside?" Calypso asks.

"It's a bunker. I took out anything rotten shortly after buying the land. You want to see?"

She nods.

I turn over a rock to pick up the key that fits the padlock I put on the door. The hinges squeak as I ease it open. Light beams in, but I still extract a flashlight from my pack to shine around.

A metal cot sits on one wall next to a set of shelves. A few interesting items remain there, mainly for posterity. An old metal case full of first aid items. A bucket with three K-ration boxes from World War II. An axe and a long, blunted sword.

An iron stove with a jaunty pipe poking through the concrete sits to one side.

Calypso sits on the cot base, laughing when it groans under her weight. "It's neat. I guess if there's a zombie apocalypse, you can ride it out here."

"We could indeed." I flash the light around, making sure nothing unexpected has happened, but everything is tight and dry. "You want to head up?"

She stands. "Sure!"

We wander back outside, and I lock up the bunker and stick the key back under the rock.

"Smart," she says. "In case the zombies are coming and you don't have time to stop by your house."

"A real prepper would add water and a generator."

"You're too much of an optimist to worry about the apocalypse."

She's probably right. We circle the bunker to a ladder that runs up the side. I've scaled it many times to assure its strength. I leave the backpack at the base. "If you feel unsure, let me know, and we'll go right back down."

"It looks fun."

But this is coming from a woman who went on an employee hike she wasn't ready for. I watch her closely as we climb the ladder. She seems good, pausing every few rungs to look out.

When we get to the top of the concrete bunker, there's another ladder up to the tower.

"We'll be able to see the castle from up here," I tell her.

"Ooooh." She follows close behind.

When I make it to the trapdoor to the walkway, I push it up and pull myself into position. Then I turn to help her.

She seems shaky for a moment, but I get her to the metal railing and she holds on as she looks out. "Oh, this is amazing."

The mountains stretch out in every direction. The highway far below is only a thin ribbon in the unbroken beauty of the trees and cliffs.

"Is that the castle?" Calypso points in the distance at the turrets.

"It is." I watch her face as she takes it all in.

I sit on the wood planks, hooking my arms over the

rail. She follows suit. We have a decent amount of walkway before the bent metal shears off where the structure took a tumble.

"Where is the rest of the tower?" she asks.

I twist to point behind us. "It fell off that ridge."

"I can't imagine being up here in a storm."

"It's how they spotted forest fires. Lightning is the most common cause."

She wraps her arms around the rail. "And what if they saw one? It would have taken forever to go somewhere to warn people."

"They used carrier pigeons. Fastened a note to their feet."

Calypso smiles. "That's clever."

"I'm glad you're not afraid of heights."

"Me, too. I felt a little unsettled on the ladder, but up here, I'm fine."

I wrap my arm around her. "This is one of my favorite places to be."

She turns and lifts her chin, and my mouth seeks hers.

This is perfect.

24

CALYPSO

Making out with Axel in the full sun on a mountainside tower is the biggest, most natural high I can imagine.

His mouth seeks mine, drawing in my breath, both familiar and somehow new at the same time.

His arms wrap around me, drawing me close to him on the platform. Our legs dangle over the edge, but we fall back onto the wood plank, smooth and worn with weather and time.

He rolls me beneath him, keeping me safe and away from the edge in his protective embrace. He has all the experience here. I trust no storm will come. No threat will arrive. He will know where the boundaries are, and no matter what happens next, I will not fall.

His body pressed on mine betrays his need for me. I can feel it hard against my thighs. I remember seeing him standing naked on the trail that first time and have to bite back a smile.

But Axel feels it. "What?" His whisper brushes my skin.

I shake my head. I don't want to disrupt this moment. I reach for his head and draw him back to my mouth.

He kisses me longer, deeper, then begins to travel. His mouth moves along my cheekbone, near my ear, and down my neck.

The sun is too bright to open my eyes after having them closed for so long, so I take in the feel of him, strong and stalwart over me. His back muscles are chiseled, shifting as he takes a path to my collarbone.

He can't get much farther in my sweatshirt, so he trails a hand down my side, easing his fingers beneath the edge. When he grazes my belly, I suck in a breath.

"Is this all right?" His mouth is back near my ear.

"Yes." I want his hands on me. I'm practically burning with the need to move forward, to fall into him.

His thumb bumps along my ribs until it reaches the elastic edge of my bra. It's nothing heavy-duty, just satin and lace. As his fingers brush over my breast, there is little in the way of each sensation. When he crosses a nipple, it puckers so tightly that I suck in a breath.

The air is cool on my exposed skin, but it's a relief from the heat rising in me. He pushes the shirt up and out of his way, easily shifting the flimsy cup of the bra to bare me to the sky.

The chill heightens the touch of his fingers, then his mouth. My back arches, my breath ragged. It's so intense. I've never felt this fevered, this alive.

His lips draw my nipple deep into his mouth, and it's

as if a string is being pulled from deep within me. Every part of my body quivers with awareness, with need.

He breaks away, and the cold is shocking and intense. I'm acutely aware of everything I'm desperate to do, where he should touch me, what I want next.

And he knows, pushing the shirt farther up my body and drawing the other breast into his mouth. I rock my pelvis into his.

He takes his time, giving this side all the attention he bestowed on the last. Molten fire creeps through me, stoking the places he's awakening. Nothing I've ever done before has come close to feeling like this.

He returns to my mouth, his kisses hot from his explorations. I crave him desperately, wondering wildly if we will do everything up here on this bare platform.

His hand returns to the breasts he abandoned. My brain wills him to move down, to touch me more.

And he gets it, his hand making its way, slipping along the outside of the sleek yoga pants.

I rock up to him, no longer caring if I seem greedy or forward. His fingers slide between my thighs, pressing into me from outside of the stretchy spandex.

It's not enough. I groan against his mouth, ready to beg.

He smiles against my mouth. "May I?"

"Yes. Yes."

He wastes no time then, dragging the elastic band low enough that he can slip a hand inside my panties.

Then one, two, three fingers are inside me.

I break the kiss, gulping in air.

He strokes me with confidence and knowledge,

experimenting to see what works, then leaning in when a long moan escapes my mouth. He's got me. Lightning bolts of pleasure start to flicker out from where he touches me.

I'm trying to hold back, not wanting to orgasm so instantly that it surprises him.

But it's too late. He flutters his hand exactly the way I need and I cry out to the trees, startling some creature who takes off in a skitter of falling leaves.

I laugh and gasp, and feel tears pop from my eyes at the same time.

Axel presses his hand firmly against me, letting the pulsing continue against his strong fingers.

I open my eyes, squinting until I can see. He's a shadowed figure against the blinding light, his eyes on me, the crinkles in the corners revealing his smile.

"I like this," he says.

I laugh again. "Do you?"

"I'd be all over you, but the condoms are way down there." He tilts his head to gesture over the edge of the tower.

So, he brought some. Interesting.

"That might be a good thing. We might fall to our deaths."

His smile extends. "Not a bad way to go."

He slowly extracts his hand from my panties and pulls up my yoga pants. "I think I had my way with you regardless."

"I think it was all *my* way."

He kisses the top of my head. "It was fun."

We sit up and I fix my bra and shirt. "I guess I better be willing to do a regular date with you now."

He rests his elbows on his knees. "I don't see why we have to do anything in an ordinary way. It's not like we met under normal circumstances."

Picturing that crash in the woods makes me grin. "That's a fact."

He jumps to his feet and takes my hand to lift me up. "Maybe dinner at my house? Then we can, perhaps, revisit what we were doing here?"

My heart hammers. Yes, I want to do to that. I want to feel this way again. In fact, I would like to do it this very minute.

But I calm myself. "I could do that."

"Good. You can see my house from here."

"Really?"

"Sure. It's closer than the castle. We only drove partway up to shorten the hike to get here."

He pulls on my hand as we walk to the edge of the platform, closer to where it falls away. "Be careful on this side."

I watch my step. He pulls me close, and we hold on to the rail as he lifts his arm. "First, find the highway. It's snaking through the trees at about two o'clock."

It takes a moment, but I spy the winding gray road.

"Follow it until you see a stone wall."

"Got it."

"You can't see the whole driveway, but it's perpendicular to the wall. It shows up in various spots."

"I see it."

"Then there will be a red roof. Some trees have lost enough leaves that you can see the pool."

My throat tightens as I find the partially hidden house in the trees. It's huge. "Is there more than one pool?"

"Well, yes. One is traditional. The other is a long lap pool. There's a third that goes indoor/outdoor. It's kind of cool. There's a wall that lowers and I can lift it and go from inside the house to outside while swimming."

Something like dread makes my stomach feel heavy. "So, you're rich."

He tries to shrug it off. "I made a fair amount off the sale of the hiking app. I don't really talk about it."

The awful feeling spreads through my body. "But you did cotillion way before that."

"Yeah, sure. We talked about that. Calypso, are you okay?"

He grew up like I did. Country club. Cotillion. Debutantes. Stuffy people trying to make their kids be like them. And now he's even richer. He probably used all his contacts. Played the game.

I bet he does charity balls. In fact, I thought that tux he wore to the haunted ball looked too fancy to be off the rack. I haven't realized how much money has played a factor in who he is because I've mostly seen him in jeans and hoodies.

I had no idea.

I hang on to the rail, moving hand over hand back to the trapdoor. I need down. I need away. I need to think.

Everything is closing in on me. The trees. The

scarred, twisted metal where the old tower fell. Axel tries to follow, but a low cry wards him off.

Jeremy was great when we first dated. He didn't try to control me, try to make me someone who fit into the society set.

But then he did. When it came down to it, rich people act certain ways to maintain their position. And this eventually included how I act when I'm with them.

So many things he's said to me sound different now. Not compliments, but where I finally met his expectations.

When I put on the red dress, "This is how you go to a ball."

Right, because before I changed, I didn't fit in.

When he chopped onions, "I can hang with anybody."

Of course! Mighty Axel bestows his presence on the lowly food service crowd.

When I talked about the Eiffel Tower, "Traveling is how you get perspective."

Because only if you have enough money to travel to other countries can you ever get perspective.

I feel sick. I need down. On the ground.

"Calypso?"

"I need to get down. Please get me down."

"Of course." He catches up. "Do you want me to go ahead or behind?"

I pause by the trapdoor. "Ahead."

He nods and pops through the opening. "There's a handle there to help you get started on the ladder."

I grab it and follow him.

We move swiftly down, then we're at the concrete roof, then descend that ladder.

I'm not sure which way to go from here, walking in small circles while Axel shoulders his backpack.

"Calypso, can you talk to me?"

I don't know what to say. "I need a minute. Can we walk back?"

"Sure, okay."

I want to tell him everything. That I was pushed for years. That his lifestyle isn't what I want. That I'm escaping the very place he's in.

I know he's different. Deep down, I really do know that.

But something's been triggered. I can't get hold of myself. My brain has re-engaged those well-worn circuits it took years for me to break.

We tromp down the trail, past the mountain cabin ruins.

Then finally, we make it to his car. I wait, my face turned to the window, while he unlocks it.

But when we're inside, he doesn't start the car. "Did I do something wrong?" He grips the steering wheel. "I pressured you, didn't I? We were up there and you couldn't get down, so you went along."

"No," I say. "No. I just didn't realize you came from money."

"Is that outside your experience? You talked about cotillion and the Eiffel Tower."

"It was my experience. Before."

His gaze takes in my face. "You escaped that life. That's why you're here."

"Something like that."

"Do you want to talk about it? Maybe I can help."

"No." I can't prevent the wavering shake in my voice.

He turns away to stare out the windshield. "I can tell you're upset. I don't want to make it worse."

We don't talk on the bumpy road to the castle. I want to say things. I want to confess that I was almost forced to marry someone, simply out of the fear of upsetting my family. That I never fit in with them. That I never fit in anywhere.

But something inside me is totally locked up. I can't find the words.

When we arrive at the employee entrance, I say, "I'm not mad. I'm not anything. I'm just…in shock. I will come out of it. I'm sorry. I'm not good with surprises. I can't. I don't."

"It's okay, Calypso." He musters a gentle look. "Text me when you're ready. I'll give you some space."

I jump out of the car, wondering if there is anything he could say, anything I could do myself, to quell the panic that's taken over.

But then he's gone, dust floating up from the path of his Land Rover.

And it doesn't matter.

25

AXEL

Well, damn.

I pull into my driveway and slam my hands on the steering wheel.

This sucks. It sucks, it sucks, it sucks.

Who knew you could be too rich?

I knew it, actually. I already struggle to trust friendships and certainly dating. Was it me they liked being around, or only my bank account?

But some people are repelled by money. Maybe someone they knew was ruined by it. Maybe it caused them harm.

And maybe they're running from someone who tried to control them with it.

It's time to Google Calypso Ash.

Decision made, I head to my office and power on my system. I've avoided looking Calypso up because I wanted to get to know the woman in front of me, not any past version.

But our relationship — if we even have one after

today — took a big leap forward. We got physical, and before she got spooked, we were about to get even more so.

I already know she's hiding things. Havannah gave me that heads up from day one. But it's time to figure out what led the most amazing woman I've met in my life to practically run from me over a nice house.

I click into the search box and put in her name.

At first there isn't much. But then I go down rabbit holes.

A few pictures line up. She's a society page debutante. Her father's a surgeon. Her mother serves on the board of some indistinct children's charity. They show up on fundraiser pages and gossip blogs, never the stars of the show, but regularly pictured with others.

I zoom in on a few of the photos. Calypso looks nothing like she does here. Her hair is styled within an inch of its life. She wears makeup at the Hollywood level. Her dresses are chic and formal and not one looks half as good as the borrowed costume from the night of the ball.

And she's miserable. I can see it. She looks like she did when I encountered her on the trail with no pants and cactus needles in private places. Lost and in pain.

I dig through the links. Once I get past the society ones, I find references to her undergrad in engineering. A project she got a student award for. Her in goggles in a group picture visiting some construction site. With some advanced digging, I spot a cached page from her old profile on LinkedIn that lists not only her engineering degree, but also that she recently worked for a civil engineering consulting firm. She had a recommendation written for her as recently as four months ago.

So she walked away from an entire career.

I figure that since I've gone this far, I might as well wade all the way in. I pony up the fee for a database search. This comes up with the address of an apartment in San Diego and a cell phone number.

It's not the contact information I have. I sign up for a new, unused Google phone number and call her old line from my computer. I'm incredibly tense to see if she'll answer, but it rolls instantly to voicemail.

And it's her all right, asking me to leave a message.

I end the call.

I scroll for a long time, but I don't find many photos of her with anyone but her parents. There's a few here and there with a guy named Jeremy Smith, but Googling him is a lost cause because the name is so common.

I stare closely at the images of the two of them together. I'm not sure they are even a couple. They never hold hands. Never look at each other. If I had to guess, they were coworkers, or he's a friend of the family.

Definitely not someone she would lose her mind with on an old fire tower.

I push away from the desk.

I was right that she grew up with money. But not sure why she'd panic over discovering I had it.

The only way I could figure that out would be through her. But clearly, she doesn't trust me enough to tell me, and we don't have enough history for her to see I'm not someone she needs to run from.

I'm back at square one with her.

I could walk away. Give up the fight.

But I'm not going to.

The brisk fall air rushes through the room as I open the side door and step out onto a balcony facing the mountains. I worked for months with the architect to make this house everything I ever wanted.

And she rejected it out of hand.

I can't quite see the fire tower from this vantage point. It gets lost in the trees. But I will not forget what happened up there. Calypso fell to pieces in my arms. We understood each other intuitively, and there is so much more to discover.

I am not going to give up on her.

If anything, I'm even more determined to make it work.

26

CALYPSO

Saturday night is long, and Sunday is no better.

I keep to my rooms. There's another new employee mixer on Sunday afternoon, indoors this time. I don't want to go. I have Netflix and a cozy mystery about a witch who solves murders.

I'm fine. Peopling gets me nowhere but exhausted.

And here I am, the assistant manager of people.

This will never work.

For the first time since I abandoned my life in San Diego, I consider going back. I have my private office at the consulting firm. I can close the door and sit with my maps and proposals and do ninety-five percent less personal interaction than I do now.

But then Jeremy would find me.

And my parents.

And I would have to clean up that big mess.

The urge to run a second time overwhelms me. Pack up. Next hostel. Next new plan.

But it occurs to me that the problem isn't my parents, or Jeremy, or my old life.

It's me.

I drag a chair to the window, staring at the mountain. Yesterday's nice weather was nothing but a warm front ahead of a cold one. It's snowing high on the peak, and the occasional drift of flakes passes by on the other side of the glass.

I'm a California girl. How am I going to handle the cold? Not with my lightweight jacket and sneakers, that's for sure. I need a real coat. And boots. And gloves. A hat. Buying them with my meager funds feels like a commitment to staying, at least through the winter.

Can I do that? With Axel so close? What do I do about him?

I can't go back.

I need a plan. I have to be frugal. Eat in my room and not at the pricy restaurant. Get warmer clothes, as cheap as I can. And only be out when I have to work. Hunker down. Watch for opportunities. Figure out what I want to do and how to get there.

Step one, shower and dress.

Two, grab a sandwich from the coffee stand.

Three, go into Boulder to find a grocery store to make eating cheaper, and outdoor wear fit for Colorado. I'm not quitting yet. If I'm careful, I can make it to the end of the year. New Year's Day will be decision day.

This feels better. I rush through the shower and blow dry my hair. I shadow my shallow lids and put on the warmest clothes I have, a thick corded sweater and a rain jacket.

By then, I'm starving, so I head downstairs, loading the Uber app while I pay for the sandwich. I should cancel my old phone. Yes, I will do that when I get back. I wonder if I can sell my car remotely. Probably not.

I've only barely set up the Uber app when I reach the counter. I set it down to order, but the woman working the stand notices the screen. "Ooh, are you going into town? I don't have anything warm enough for the weather that's about to hit."

Peopling. Uggh.

But I have to do it.

I manage a smile. "Yes. Me neither. And I need groceries."

"Me, too! Can you wait ten minutes? I'll be off and we can share the Uber. It's thirty bucks each way into town."

Thinking about saving thirty dollars isn't something I'm used to, but based on what's happening in my life at the moment, I better start.

"Sure. I'll eat my sandwich in the bar."

"Cool. I'll come find you."

Only when I'm sitting down with my turkey and Swiss do I realize I've committed to an outing with a coworker I met before, but I can't remember her name.

I sit at a low table in view of the stand, occasionally glancing at her to see if my stupid brain will come up with who she is. Lauren? Lindsey?

Wait. She went on that hike. And we got some group text about where to meet.

I take a big bite of the sandwich and scroll back through my texts. My heart stutters for a moment when

I see Axel's name. He hasn't tried to reach me. He's kept his word to give me space.

I find the hiking text, which of course strikes another emotional hit since that was the day I met him. There were six of us. Duke. Cameron. Shelly. Aparna. Louise. That's it — Louise!

I breathe a sigh of relief. When I get the deli staff settled, I'm going to have to memorize their names immediately. I can't be in charge of people whose names I can't remember.

Something makes me scroll back through Axel's texts. There are so many, talk about bread, about pickles, Laffy Taffy jokes, meeting times. I go all the way back to the beginning, when I texted him that my taffy joke made me write him.

Had it really, though? Or had it been his charm? His kindness? His relentless chase? Hadn't he cut his finger while learning to dice with me? Taken on the humiliation of his bread failure?

What am I doing?

Acting out of fear, that's what.

The moment on the tower washes over me, making my cheeks go warm with the memory of Axel's fingers in my body and how quickly I responded.

That was something Jeremy hadn't been able to do. Not once. And the only man I'd slept with in college hadn't either.

My treacherous body tingles, like a shop door's chime to tell me I can enter now, and don't I want to peruse the delights inside?

And I do. I really do.

Louise approaches my table, pulling on her jacket and unrolling the long black braid she had tucked in her cap. "You want me to call the first one?"

"I can do it," I say, and tap on the destination I already set, a hike and ski shop on the outskirts of town.

"Oh, I've heard this store is good," she says. "They have a great clearance section."

"Perfect." It's odd talking about sales. Mother would rather die than buy something marked down.

My phone buzzes. "Looks like someone got dropped off at the castle and the driver picked up our ride. They're out front."

"Awesome." Louise waits while I re-wrap my sandwich and stick it in my pocket.

Then we're out of the castle and driving along the twisting entryway.

"I haven't left the grounds since we got hired two weeks ago," Louise says.

I've only left to go hiking with Axel, but I don't want to mention that. "It's easy to stay, other than needing to eat something different from their food."

"It's good," Louise says, "but it's expensive."

I nod.

"How big of a coat do you think we need? I'm from Louisiana and we barely need a coat two days a year, if that."

"I'm from San Diego. Same."

Louise laughs. "We should have brought someone who knows Colorado."

"Hopefully someone at the shop can help."

"You're right." Louise picks at a loose thread on her

artfully ripped jeans. "I guess I'm used to Target and Walmart where you're on your own."

I wish I could say, "Same," but I've never shopped at either place. Not that I buy my own things. Hardly ever. Mother has always controlled my wardrobe. And all the gifts I got for my birthday or Christmas or any other occasion, from pearls to clothes to bags and scarves, were pointedly contrived to ensure I had all the proper ensembles for when I saw her.

I do have some outfits of my own, sweats and yoga pants, and I particularly love T-shirts with puns on them. I'm currently wearing one that says "Muffin compares to you."

In fact, my own clothes were the only ones I brought, although I did pack them in a Louis Vuitton suitcase, which raised some eyebrows at the hostel I stayed at, at least by the few people there who knew what that meant. It's currently hidden in the bottom of my closet.

We approach civilization. I stayed in Boulder the night before my first day at the castle, so I know the route. The car turns into the parking lot of the Hike 'n Ski.

Louise grabs her purse and hauls herself out. "I sure hope they have something." She watches the flurries coming down. "I hear this is only the beginning."

It's noticeably colder now than when we left the castle. A storm is blowing in. We hurry into the store, then both stop at the sheer overwhelm.

Hike 'n Ski is huge. There's a fake mountain in the

center of the store, and kids are going down a slide from the top.

"Whoa," Louise says. "I had no idea it was so big." She rushes past a display of snow boots to the stairs of the mountain.

She disappears for a moment, then I spot her pink jacket as she shouts, "Wheeee," on her way down.

She lands with a thump at the bottom of the slide.

A five-year-old side-eyes her. "Aren't you too big to be on this slide?"

"I'm faster than you." Louise takes off for the stairs again, the girl on her tail.

I'm definitely learning something about my coworker.

Signposts identify the four sections of the store. We're in the ski section. There are coats here, but one glance at a price tag tells me we better find that clearance section. I would have hesitated to pay that much even at my old job.

There's a camping section with tents and cookware and sleeping bags. Then a hiking section, with an entire shoe department plus packs and walking sticks and clothing for all weather types.

Another area is simply called outdoor adventure. There's a wall of bikes and helmets and rows of rock climbing equipment. Several people repel down a towering wall fitted with footholds.

"Looking for anything in particular?" A burly guy with a plaid shirt and a man bun startles me.

"Oh," I say. "My friend is on her third round of going down the slide."

We watch Louise and the girl race another time to the stairs.

"They're having a good time. Let me know if you need anything."

I nod. I guess I could have asked him where the clearance section is, but I'm finding it hard to silence the long-engrained voices in my head. My mom in particular keeps saying, "Never settle for last season."

When Louise arrives at the bottom of the slide a fourth time, I approach her. "I'm going to go look around."

"Sure!" Her eyes are bright, as if this is the best time she's had in a while.

The girl takes advantage of the delay and makes it to the stairs ahead of her.

"Dang it! I'll see you there. Just one more slide."

I laugh. "All right."

And she's off.

Everything is bright and shiny as I wander through the ski section to the opposite side of the mountain. I spot a yellow "Clearance" sign on the back wall and head for it.

It's mostly summer things, shorts and water shoes and tank tops, but there's a rack of coats. I'm thumbing through them, not sure there's anything that will work for me, when Louise rushes up. "Did you see the price on those ski jackets? I may have to go to Walmart."

I hold up a bright pink puffy coat that matches Louise's current light jacket. "This seems to be your color."

"Ooooh." Louise drops her purse to the ground and

shoves an arm in the sleeve. "It's so warm!" She zips it up and walks up to a mirrored column, turning from side to side.

"I like it," I tell her and flip through the coats once more. Other than the pink one I gave Louise, they are all dull shades of olive or brown. I guess I shouldn't worry about the color. It's mainly for when I might take walks or possibly go into town.

Not for hikes with Axel.

I'm not doing that.

Right?

I pull a green one down.

"Oh no," Louise says. "That will make you look like one of those old army figures a kid would line up in battle." She admires her pink arms.

I put it on anyway. It feels tight across the shoulders. "Doesn't fit, anyway."

There's a white one in a larger size. It's got more puff than the others. I slip it on.

Louise giggles. "And now you're a marshmallow."

I peer into the mirror. It's true.

"Bigfoot would swoop down to snag you and roast you over an open fire." Louise pulls off the coat and hugs it to her. "There's no more pink ones?"

"I don't think I'm much on pink."

A salesclerk arrives with an armful of coats. "New clearance, ladies," she says. She hangs several red coats on the rack.

"Ooooh," Louise says. "This one is nice." She holds up a tag. "Eight hundred dollars marked down to forty? What kind of crazy discount is that?"

The woman shrugs. "That's why it's called clearance." She moves to another rack and rearranges shorts.

Louise moves quickly through the new coats. "They're all too small for me." She huffs. "But I like this pink one, anyway."

I glance around, feeling prickly with suspicion. The sudden appearance of red coats wildly marked down. I glance around, sure I'll see Axel somewhere. This sounds like something a rich person would do.

But I don't see him.

I pull a red coat off a hanger, the label pronouncing it rated for subzero temperatures. It's glossy and smooth on the outside. The inside is downy soft. I slip it on. It fits like a dream. I zip it up and look in the mirror.

"If there was a skiwear competition for Miss America, you would be wearing that," Louise says. "You've got to get it."

I nod. "I think I will." I slide the coat off and hang it up again. "Thanks."

"I'll check you out," the salesclerk says. "Come with me."

Interesting. We bypass the line and head to customer service. She charges Louise for her coat, then turns to me. "Ready?"

"Sure." I look around again, feeling suspicious. Still no Axel.

Maybe I'm wrong. But this seems like his kind of place. And if he spotted me, I would totally believe that he told this woman he'd pay for the coat and to charge me something small.

The coat rings up for the forty dollars plus tax. I pay in cash.

"Thank you so much, ladies!" The woman hands me the bag.

I watch her as we walk away. She hurries back to the clearance section.

"Hold on a sec," I tell Louise. "I want to check something."

And sure enough, the clerk takes the rest of the red coats off the display.

Yup. I knew it.

I'm tempted to climb the mountain and look for him, but Louise is waiting.

I find her standing by the door, pulling off the tags. "This was great. Oh! We forgot to call the Uber."

"The grocery store isn't far. Should we test out our coats?"

Louise peers into the afternoon sky. "It stopped snowing. Why not?"

We both put on our new finds and stuff our old lightweight jackets in the bags.

And as we walk through the parking lot to cut through to the next shopping center, which includes a small grocer, I see exactly what I suspected I might, parked in the center of a row.

A green Land Rover.

Axel.

I don't know whether to be mad or grateful.

Probably both.

27

AXEL

As I leave the parking lot of Hike 'n Ski, I don't know if I did the right thing at the store.

Seeing Calypso there did something weird to me. She looked at price tags. She frowned. She headed to the clearance section. She found nothing.

Yes, I stalked her.

Not *to* the store. I was there for a rock climbing lesson. But from the top of the wall, I saw all these things, hanging onto the handholds so long that my instructor thought I was stuck.

So yes, I bought all the red coats and instructed the salesperson to charge only a small amount. We donated the rest.

Then I imagined her finding out that I did it and being mad.

When I sold my app, I thought the money was the best thing to happen to me. I never had to work again. I could buy land, support conservation efforts, and do great things with it.

Then everyone I ever knew wanted to be my best friend. Women draped themselves over me. I had only one shot at getting to know someone and figure out if they were genuine, because by a second meeting, they knew who I was and my net worth.

Now, I'm pretty sure this fortune is the worst thing. I limit myself to family these days, because they're the only people I trust. I hide out on a mountain and use my accountant's office to field business calls because everyone wants something from me.

And Calypso, the one person I got to know free of all that baggage, hates me for it.

I put through a call to my accountant. It's a Sunday, but he's an old family friend.

"Axel! How are you?"

"I want to donate the whole thing."

"What do you mean, the whole thing?"

"All the money. I want less than a million. Pay off the house. Create some fund for the taxes and upkeep. Then leave less than a million in the bank."

There's silence on the other end.

"Ben?"

He clears his throat. "First of all, your money isn't all liquid."

"Then liquify it."

"There will be penalties. Fees. Selling all your stock might create upheaval in a few of the portfolios."

"I don't care."

"Axel, what's this about?"

"I'm sick of it. Sick of what it means."

"What it means to have this level of wealth?"

"It has a price."

"Have you talked to anyone about this?"

"No one. I trust nobody. That's the problem. I'll find a job. Be a regular person again."

"This isn't an unusual feeling. People who win the lottery go through a lot of the same feelings."

"Get rid of it, Ben. I don't want it."

"I'll prepare a draft report of what it will take to do it. Then we can have a meeting to discuss all the implications."

"Good. Thank you."

"Talk to some people first, Axel," he says. "Isn't Donovan McDonald near you? He'd be a good one. He's been where you are."

Has he? His net worth is five times mine. "Okay."

"We'll touch base again when I've done some research."

"All right."

I toss the phone on the seat.

But then I wonder if I give it all away, will it even matter? Calypso wouldn't know. I might still be the thing she's running from.

I pull over at a gas station. I want to shed some of this and see how it feels.

My second choice for this year's hefty donation was an environmental charity. I pull up their website and hit their donation button.

I put in one million, but it spits back an error.

Right. It doesn't believe me.

I incrementally bring it down until it accepts a

ninety-nine-thousand-dollar figure. It only takes credit cards.

I use my no-limit card, and as soon as the transaction hits the card, I pay it off with my personal bank account.

I immediately get a fraud alert.

Good grief. Why is this so damn hard?

I call both the credit card and the bank to assure them that yes, I did intend to donate that much and to ignore any fraud for the rest of the day.

Then I do it again. Ninety thousand to a homeless shelter. Ninety thousand to a food bank. Ninety thousand to an endangered species nonprofit. Ninety thousand to an organization for domestic violence.

After an hour of sitting idle at the gas station, I feel better. I just shed almost half a million dollars.

But it probably won't make a difference. There's still over four hundred million to go.

My car is covered with snow. I crank my wipers and take off down the highway. As I approach the road to the castle, it takes a lot of effort to pass it without turning in.

I don't even know if Calypso is there. She and the other woman walked over to the grocery store.

I'm so unsettled.

The snowfall gets heavier as I drive home. Once there, though, I sit in my garage, not sure what to do next.

Then a car pulls into my driveway.

I get out of the Land Rover and walk out of the garage.

It's Mom. She waves and opens her door. "I have casseroles for the only child of mine who likes my cooking!"

She walks to the passenger side looking like a carrot in her long pale orange coat. Mom always likes the oddest color combinations.

When she opens the door, she steps back so I can collect the stack of casserole dishes on the floorboard. There's three of them.

"How much did you cook?"

"Oh, only a little. There's an eggplant lasagna, a beet pie, and split pea polenta."

"They sound delicious." Even as I say it, I can picture Rhett and Court falling to the floor, even as grown-ass adults, acting like they're being poisoned.

We go through the garage to enter the house. Mom surveys the two empty bays. "Are you going to buy cars for those, or are you hoping to find someone else to park here?"

Subtle. "Helps the resale value to build out a decent garage."

"So you won't live here forever?"

"Don't have a crystal ball on me."

"Hmmmph." She frowns with her signature mom sound. "A birdie told me that maybe you have a sweetheart."

A sweetheart. I imagine Calypso making a dartboard with the word on it and piercing each letter with a menacing throw.

We enter the kitchen and I set the casseroles on the counter near the fridge. "Who blabbed?"

"A mother never reveals her sources." She pulls off her gloves as she glances around. "Looks like the cleaning crew did a good job. When are they coming back?"

"Every Monday."

"Excellent. Can't have you scaring off this young lady with your bachelor ways."

I ignore this, rearranging a shelf to accommodate the casserole dishes.

Mom wanders into the living room, presumably to check on the work the cleaners did there. I lean against the counter, gathering my patience. She cares, that's all. She's not trying to make me uncomfortable.

When I enter the room with soaring windows that perfectly frame the new snowfall, she's sitting on the sofa. "This view," she says. "Forget your father. I'm going to live with you."

"Can I make you some coffee?"

"Tea, dear. If I drink coffee after noon, I won't sleep." She holds out an arm to stop me. "But before you go, you should know that this young woman is the talk of all the Pickles. I heard you two were alone in the pantry the whole time Sherman and his boys were setting up the new deli."

I figured that was the source. I wonder if it was Anthony who ratted me out, or maybe Uncle Sherman himself. "We were. There's not much to tell. We haven't even gone on a date."

"Oh. I see. Everyone felt you two were very… familiar with each other."

"We like each other's company. Not sure it will go anywhere." And certainly not now.

"Go start the tea. Then tell your old meddling mother everything."

I head to the kitchen. I should have known her visit had multiple purposes. She's never directly asked me about my dating life, not even when I lived at home. But then, I'm not sure anyone lasted long enough to get on her radar. A few girls came to our house in high school, but I never brought anyone home from college.

And since the app sale, it's harder to find someone who isn't primarily interested in my bank account. Some of them try to be casual about it, but eventually there's a carefully dropped hint about always wanting to go to Barbados. Or I'm stopped in front of the window of a jewelry shop.

And all my hope crashes to the floor.

The electric kettle has finished its cycle by the time I collect the mugs and sugar. I pour water over the tea bags of our shared favorite cinnamon spice and bring the burnished wood tray with mugs and spoons and sugar into the living room.

"Lovely," Mom says. "This beautiful view and my nearest boy bringing me tea are the makings of a perfect day."

She picks up her mug, idly tugging on the string of the tea bag as it steeps. I drop into a side chair and wait her out. I'm certainly not going to volunteer any information.

"So, how did you meet her?" Mom watches the

snow, but I'm fully aware of how sharp her peripheral vision is.

"She wandered onto one of my trails after getting separated from her group."

"Oh, my! Had she been lost long?"

"A while. I got her back."

"You were her hero!"

I picture Calypso in the dirt, and my own swinging cock. Yeah, no heroes. "Not really."

"Wait, you weren't naked, were you?"

I hesitate a second too long.

"Axel Rose Armstrong! You will promise your mother that you will only go out on the trails in decent attire!" She's definitely got her eyes on me, and that look is one that could send me scurrying to my room when I was a kid.

It still might.

But I'm not making her that promise.

"Don't forget your sugar," I tell her, leaning forward to drop a cube in my mug.

"Hmmmph." She tugs the tea bag out of her mug to rest on a saucer. "So, even after that unexpected meeting, she was willing to talk to you?"

I skip the day I went to the castle looking for her. "Havannah made me the ghoul in the Haunted Ball, and Calypso ran the spotlight."

"Calypso." Mom considers the name. "Where is she from?"

"California."

"How did she end up here?"

"She was looking for a change." I'm making an

assumption, but I can't let that question have too much weight by not giving an answer.

"It is nice here. Sometimes I miss New York, but I like this, too."

"She bought a coat at Hike 'n Ski today." I don't know why I throw in this random detail, other than maybe to feel like we're still full of possibilities.

"Well, it sounds like a nice romance. Does she like your house?"

I know a fishing expedition when I hear one. "She's only seen it from the trail. We went up to the fire tower two days ago, the warm day."

"So she's an adventurer like you, then?" She seems pleased.

"She's learning."

Mom nods. "Does she know about your app?"

"I showed it to her."

"But not about your situation."

This renders me silent again. I don't know how to explain what happened.

"Axel?"

"I'm getting rid of it."

"Getting rid of what?"

"The money. I dumped half a million in the parking lot of the gas station, and Ben is liquidating everything."

She sits straight up. "Why would you do that?"

"Because it's been the worst thing."

She moves to the end of the sofa to sit closer. "But this beautiful house! Your freedom to do hikes whenever you like!"

"And no genuine friends anymore. And women who are hoping I don't insist on a prenup."

Mom sets her mug down. "How did Calypso react?"

"She left me. I don't know exactly why. She didn't realize I had money."

"I see. So because of this one woman, you're going to throw away the fruits of all your hard work."

I lay my head back on the chair and stare at the steepled roof. "I don't know. Probably it won't do any good."

"I thought you were giving it all away slowly, anyway."

"I'm speeding up the process."

She's quiet for a while, then finally she says, "Money isn't evil in itself. What it does is amplify whatever issues you already had. If you were greedy, you'll be more so. If you wanted power, you use it to get more."

Her hand lands on mine, and I look at her. "But if you were already kind and careful, you'll have the opportunity to use those traits on a bigger scale. So I think giving it away is a good move for you, but take your time. Don't let your tendency to be impatient be the part of you that gets amplified."

She's right. I have been in a hurry to solve a problem, and I may not have gone about it the right way.

"Okay, Mom."

We sit with this for a while, and she seems satisfied. The snow keeps falling, and we sip our tea. Then her phone buzzes. "That's your dad. He wants me home before the snow piles too high." She sets her mug on the tray. "Enjoy your casseroles. I hope you get a chance to share one with your lady."

That's unlikely, but I don't tell her that.

I walk her out the front to her car. She kisses my cheek, the snow quickly frosting her hair white. "I know you will make all the right choices."

As she turns around and heads down the driveway, I back up to the porch, appreciating the cold and the way the new snow blankets the trees.

Normally I like winter, but this one already feels cold and bleak.

28

CALYPSO

The snow is really coming down. I drink my morning coffee, watching the flakes softly blanket the mountains. Everything is white.

In half an hour, I get to meet my new staff. I submitted my choices to Filo, and he approved them all. They will all be notified this morning, and we will convene in the new deli to assign roles.

It feels good. It's a new and interesting challenge, leading a crew.

I got a few things in order yesterday. The grocery store had a small branch of a local bank, so I opened an account and deposited my first check.

I'm committed to being here, Axel or no Axel, for the rest of the year.

I checked my old email and responded only to my sister, saying I had a job and was settled.

There were dozens of messages from my mother and probably a hundred or more from Jeremy.

I didn't read them.

I'm not ready.

My phone beeps to tell me it's time to go down. I love how clean and empty the screen is. No email. No social media apps. Just a calendar and clock and weather. I like looking at the screen with Boulder on the top and the image of snow falling.

I purposefully escaped and simplified so I could determine my future without anyone's pressure.

Axel was a complication I didn't need.

I tie on my apron over my Tasty Pickle T-shirt and fix my hat to my hair with bobby pins. Shadow the shallow eyelids.

And done.

I take the stairs down to the lobby and wave at Filo's son, who waits by a stack of luggage on a rolling cart. When I arrive half an hour early at the deli, Havannah and Filo are already there, printouts spread in front of them on the chopping block.

"Hey, Calypso," Havannah says. "We're reviewing the assignments and your notes."

I step beside them. "I ranked their skill levels plus my hunch about their ability to improve and enjoy certain tasks, especially the trickier ones like bread baking."

Havannah runs a finger along a column. "You even noted who was a morning person."

"The bread baking shift starts at six a.m. Some people are not at their best that early." My belly quivers. I'm not sure if Havannah likes my attention to detail or if she thinks I'm too much.

"I like it," she says, and I release a breath. "Since

the deli is only open until two, we can't accommodate the night owls, but we'll at least be informed." She collects the pages and stacks them. "Shall we get out the uniforms and badges so everyone can look the part?"

I nod, heading to the pantry where the boxes of T-shirts and aprons and hats are waiting. On top is a plastic baggie of badges I haven't seen before. I open it and find mine. *Calypso Ash. Assistant Manager.*

Despite my conflicted emotions about using my degree, I'm proud. My old job might have appeared to have more stature, but really, I was at the bottom of the pile in our project groups. I got to check the math, type up the reports, and organize the files, but I was never the one who made the math, designed the report, or prepared the data for the files.

Here, I make almost all the decisions. Who to hire. When to schedule them. What specials to run. What to order.

The new employees arrive, nervous and chattering. Havannah welcomes each of them with a smile and a handshake. Filo tells them their assignment and work schedule for the week. I fit them in their outfits and send them to the bathroom down the hall to change.

Then, they're all assembled and Havannah leaves us to it. Filo takes aside the choppers and bakers for prep work. I instruct the others to lightly fill the assembly line. Everyone will eat in the deli today, and we will practice on each other.

Soon the bins are filling with deli meats, cheese, condiments, vegetables, and pickles. Bread is baking. I take aside three employees to review the order system and register.

We eat and critique. Too much mustard, too little mayo. Onion slices too thick. Shake the juice off before placing a pickle on a plate. Details can improve the experience.

Louise glances around. "Where's Axel? I thought he was going to work with us?"

Everyone turns to me.

My mouth goes dry around my bite of sourdough. I can only shrug.

"Someone should text him," says Aparna, a local teen paying for college by working at the castle.

"He's rich," Duke says. He's wearing basketball shorts even though it's snowing. "Why would he be here?"

"Not as rich as he was," Louise says, picking up her phone. "Did you see the Buzzfeed article about him this morning? He apparently gave away half a million dollars yesterday."

I sit up straight at that. He did? Yesterday? Before or after he arranged for my red coat?

Aparna launches out of her seat to look at Louise's screen. "Holy shit. He did. He started maxing out their donation boxes. The IT guy for one of the charities says Axel tried to donate a million to them, but their system flagged it as fake so it wouldn't go through."

Filo catches my eye, but I avoid any incriminating glances. Why did he do that? And why yesterday? Because of my upset that he was rich?

Filo claps his hands. "All right, everyone, back to it.

Switch roles from this morning. We need as many people knowing as many things as possible before the grand opening."

"When's the first real day?" Louise asks.

"When we are ready!" Filo stands up. "Duke and Aparna, clear the tables and refill the ice bin over the soda fountain. I know we didn't use many cups, but practice locating the right sizes and replenishing stock. Everyone else, learn something new this afternoon."

I follow him back to the kitchen. I want to text Axel and ask what's going on with him. Surely he won't try giving away all of his money because of me.

As I try to come up with the right thing to say, it all sounds ridiculous. I don't know anything about what motivates him. I can't assume I have any influence.

But as we resume baking the various breads, I have to wonder, what if it's true? If he sacrificed his entire fortune for me, what would I do about it?

29

AXEL

Havannah texts me Monday night.

Thought you'd be at the deli for the first
official training day. Trouble with
Calypso?

I haven't left my living room all day. Watching the snowfall has been a beautiful distraction from my chaotic thoughts.

Me: Calypso asked for some space.

Havannah: Good for you for giving it
to her.

I stare at the line for a moment. It's not good for me. But it's good for her.

Me: Did it go well?

Havannah: So far! Everyone got along
and was practicing their roles.

I want to ask after Calypso. I want every detail. Did she laugh any? Or did that line between her eyebrows get deep? Did she talk to the others easily? Or was she spending time in the pantry to collect herself?

But Havannah's on to me. She makes it easy.

> Havannah: She worked well and was friendly. But she definitely wasn't the same as I've seen her with you. Is it fixable?
>
> Me: I don't know.
>
> Havannah: Let us know if we can help.

I remember my accountant telling me I should talk to Donovan.

> Me: Ben said I should talk to Don.
>
> Havannah: For financial advice?
>
> Me: Something like that.
>
> Havannah: We're having dinner after the restaurant closes tonight. Late. After ten. You want to come?

To the castle. Where Calypso works.

> Me: But, space.
>
> Havannah: You can come in through the back. I'll make sure it's clear.
>
> Me: Okay. Thanks.

I set down my phone. This is good. I can't safely hike in this weather, and little else gets me out of the house these days. If it looks hopeless with Calypso, maybe I'll go visit Rhett or Court. Get out of town. I could join a hiking expedition in South America. Somewhere it's not snowing. I can do anything.

Even though I'm not supposed to see Calypso, I dress like I might pass her in the hall. This takes some thought. I can't look dressed up. That would emphasize what she hates about me.

I choose black jeans, dressier than blue ones but still not fancy. A green sweater, nothing expensive, just a Hike 'n Ski zipper-front. I go with hiking boots. Then sneakers. Then boots again.

When I back out of my garage, I'm glad for the Land Rover. My drive is getting deep with snow. I'll have to call out a plow service if this keeps up.

Or maybe I'll shovel the whole quarter mile by hand. That'll keep me busy.

It's a quick shot down the highway to the castle. Havannah has already had the long, winding drive plowed. She'll probably do it every few days to keep it clear.

Now that the Haunted Ball is over, the castle will be considerably less busy. High season is done. Even so, the parking lot is fuller than I would have thought. I drive around to the back and take a spot near the new barn.

When I emerge from the car, I hear the distinct hee-haw of the donkeys. I'm about ten minutes early, so I walk up to the pens.

They are empty of livestock and blanketed with fresh snow. But light shines out from the open doors.

I hop the fence and head to the entrance.

Vincent is there, plus the gray-haired caretaker from Avalonia. Most of the donkeys are in their stalls, but they have one out in a makeshift pen made of mesh chicken wire. She's fat-bellied, her body heaving.

Vincent looks up, his five o'clock shadow dark on his cheeks. "Hey, Axel. You're here late."

"Having dinner with Havannah and Donovan."

He nods. "Got us a trickster here. Nobody knew she was pregnant when they shipped her."

The gray-haired man pats her head. "Gonna sit with her while she labors."

"Is she in any trouble?" I ask.

"Oh, no. Looks right as rain," the man says. "Just didn't have a maternity pen set up. Didn't think we'd need it. This wasn't a breeding group."

I bend down to stroke the lady's head. "Labor well," I tell her. "Looks like she's in good hands. G'night."

"Don't stay too long," Vincent says. "Weatherman says the snow will stay light, but my old knees say it's comin' on a blizzard."

I grin. His knees know better than meteorologists. Right. "I'll keep that in mind."

I head to the rear of the castle. It's locked up this late, but I hit the buzzer and one of the cook staff lets me in. "Havannah and Donovan are in the private space off the main dining room," the woman says.

"Thanks." My chest feels tight as I head through the back halls. Calypso should be well ensconced in her wing by now, but even so, I'm in her domain.

I shouldn't have worried. I don't pass a soul as I

enter the back side of the restaurant and cross over to the only private dining room with the lights on.

Donovan and Havannah sit at a table, her son Rebel curled up in Mickey Mouse pajamas, asleep on her lap.

"Sorry about the intruder," Havannah says. "He wouldn't go down, so I brought him."

I sit across from them. "Must be something, growing up in a castle."

She ruffles his hair. "Yeah, sometimes I wonder if this isn't ideal. It's not a normal childhood."

"He'll be fine," Donovan says. "And if it feels off when he turns five and starts school, we'll think about buying a house in town."

A server pushes a cart with several silver domes into the room.

"We're having a pasta night," Havannah says. "I needed some comfort food."

"Sounds great," I say.

Three white plates are set in front of us, then several steaming dishes of various pastas. My stomach rumbles.

Rebel lurches awake. "Is that a thunderstorm, Mama?"

She laughs quietly. "No, little one. That's Uncle Axel's hungry tummy."

I press my hand to my belly. "Sorry."

Rebel closes his eyes again. "Sounds like a monster is in there."

"Could be," I say.

Havannah bites back a smile.

Donovan spoons her servings of linguini and gnocchi. I take a heaping helping of fettuccini Alfredo.

The server fills our water glasses, then leaves us.

Donovan spins his fork in his linguini. "Havannah says you wanted some advice."

"I want to hear this," Havannah says, reaching over Rebel to stab a bite. "Everyone's talking about the half a mil you dropped on charities yesterday."

My fork goes still halfway to my mouth. "What?"

Donovan touches his phone and shifts screens. Then he turns it around. "You're now the world's most eligible philanthropist."

I scan the article. Some tech worker tipped off the story after noticing my failed million. Once that broke, the other charities chimed in with the donations I made from my car.

I slide the phone back to Donovan. "Isn't that supposed to be private?"

"When you use their public-facing web portals, there's an option to donate anonymously, but the default is to list your name on a patron page. You're on all of them. Rookie mistake."

"I did it in a hurry."

"You should have donations that size go through your accountant. The credit card company got some hefty fees that could have gone to the charity."

"Right." I twiddle with the pasta.

"It's all right, Axel," Havannah says. "I'm as new to this game as you are. What prompted that big donation spree?"

I avoid the question by shoving a bite in my mouth.

Havannah glances at Donovan. "I think I'll go put this one to bed. I'll be back if I can."

"Should I send up the food?" Donovan asks.

"Oh, it's coming with me." She dumps another heap of gnocchi on her plate, then expertly stands, adjusts Rebel on her hip, and picks up her plate. "See you in a while, hopefully."

We eat in silence for a few minutes, then Donovan sits back. "You know I grew up poor, right?"

"No."

"Back in the day, my brother Dell Brant was Hasmund McDonald."

I'd wondered why they had different last names, but I never asked.

Donovan sets his napkin neatly by his plate. "We worked at the greyhound racetrack, mucking out stalls."

"Really?"

"Yep. My parents still work there."

"Why?"

"They don't want to be rich. They like their trailer, their friends, and their jobs. Dad keeps the hot dog stands stocked as a runner. Mom is a waitress."

"But they could live anywhere, do anything."

"It's not what they want."

I hadn't changed my parents' lifestyle either. I offered, but they already did well. Mom let me take her to Paris on a private plane, though. Not my own. I don't need one. But I commissioned a jet for hire.

"How did you go from mucking stalls to this?" I gesture to the castle.

"This was a gift to my bride," Donovan says. "My brother blazed the trail. Corporate investments. Banking. Buying and selling companies. You leverage yourself to the eyeballs and hope for the best."

"I sold an app."

"Tech millionaires are a wild bunch. Most of them will blow it all within a decade or less. Do you have a mentor?"

"No."

"You should."

"Nobody told me."

"There isn't a playbook for this." Donovan sips his water. "So, what brought on the donations? Did something trigger you?"

I glance at the door.

"Havannah and I don't have secrets, but I don't have to tell her everything."

I shrug. "It's fine. I have a hard time trusting my judgement about people. Who's real. Who's in it for positioning near me."

He nods. "Common problem. It can take time to sharpen those instincts. Did something specific happen?"

"Calypso. She found out about the money."

"And she didn't like it."

"No. Totally spooked her."

Donovan turns the glass in circles. "Interesting. So, you were hoping to impress her with your philanthropy?"

"I was trying to get rid of it."

He laughs. "That's harder to do than you think. Your fortune probably isn't readily available, not if you used a financial advisor."

"That's what my accountant said."

"How did the conversation go with Calypso?"

"It wasn't much of one. She saw my house, realized I was rich, and said she needed space. That she was in shock."

"And no indication if she would come back to you?"

"No."

"And she's worth giving away your entire fortune? How long have you known her?"

I sink in my chair. "Two weeks."

"I'm not going to judge you for that. I knew Havannah was the one for me after two hours."

"Would you give up your fortune for her?"

"No. I might change my lifestyle. I would certainly try to live more like she does. But I'd get to the real problem. Money isn't the actual issue."

And there it is. What Mom said.

"Okay. I get it."

"I don't disagree with the path you're taking. Many billionaires take a pledge to donate half of their net worth in their lifetime. No one would expect it of you, not with a one-off windfall. But a life of philanthropy is never a bad thing. Do it for the right reasons."

I stare past him at the tall windows flanked with gold curtains. The snow is so heavy that the night sky is white. "It's coming down."

Donovan turns. "It wasn't supposed to be a white-out."

Both of our phones buzz at the same time.

Weather alert: Blizzard conditions.

"They're going to close the highway," Donovan says. "If you want to make it home, you better go."

"Nonsense." Havannah breezes into the room. "You're not going anywhere in this. If I'd known it was coming, I never would have invited you. We'll give you a room, and you can assess the situation in daylight."

Great. Now I'm spending the night here. "I can't run into Calypso."

Havannah pins me with a look. "Axel, this castle has four wings and three hundred rooms. Stay away from the deli, and you won't see her."

"Okay. Got it."

She peers into the dishes. "Sit down. We have more pasta to knock back. I'll have someone bring you a room key."

Before I can think about it, I say, "Can I have the secret suite?"

Her eyes go wide. "How do you know about that?"

Shoot. I don't want to get Calypso in trouble.

"I plead the fifth."

"That suite is only for the rare person I deem worthy of the secret." She seems miffed. "But I suppose you'll do."

"High praise."

She realizes she doesn't have a plate anymore and stabs a bite of Donovan's pasta. "Don't push your luck. And I'll get it out of you how you know about it. I assume you know how to get to it?"

"I do."

"I'll key your card myself. Even the front desk

doesn't know about that suite." She stabs another bite, then heads out of the room again.

I lean back into the chair. "I guess I'm staying here."

"And Calypso is in the building," Donovan says.

Don't I know it.

30

CALYPSO

We're lucky most of the staff lives on site, because a blizzard hits overnight and no one can get in or out of the castle. Filo can't come in, so I'm in charge of the second day with the new deli employees.

Without Filo's oppressive presence, everyone is energetic and eager. We all enjoy slowly preparing the entire menu.

Duke finds a jar of ghost pepper pickles in the pantry and breaks them out, daring everyone to try a slice.

"Nobody feel like you have to eat it," I say, stopping short of telling them I had the most fiery kiss in the history of kisses after eating the relish version. "And make the slices thin."

Hopefully, only a small amount won't be as traumatic. Clearly, the other delis sell these pickles regularly.

Louise volunteers first, her dark eyes flashing fear as she watches Duke cut the pickle. "Am I going to die?"

Duke slides a slice across the chopping block with the knife. "It will only kill a few of your taste buds."

Louise picks up the piece. "I can feel the heat on my skin!"

"Eat it!" Aparna says. "Before it burns your hand."

"I don't think it will burn her hand," I say.

"Wait!" Duke says, and pulls his phone out. "For posterity." He starts recording.

Louise stares at the pickle balanced on the tip of her finger, her long braid hanging below her Tasty Pickle cap. She looks scared.

But she closes her eyes, opens her mouth and pops the slice inside.

Then her eyes fly open. "Oh, no!"

"Milk," Duke says. "Get her some milk!"

Aparna flies to the fridge and pulls out a jug. "Get a cup!" she shouts.

I'm the closest to the dining area, so I race to the soda dispenser and pull a cup from the stack.

Aparna meets me halfway and dumps milk into it and runs it to Louise.

Louise's eyes are watering as she gulps the milk. After a moment, she sets down the empty cup and sucks in a breath. "I survived," she says. "Who's next?"

I think everyone will be spooked, but the whole staff crowds around the chopping block.

"Group taste!" Duke shouts, chopping more pickle. "Someone prepare the cups."

I'm not sure what Filo or Havannah would think about our ritual, but I feel like it's building camaraderie among the staff. And it might be good for customer service. If someone asks about the ghost pepper pickle, all of them can explain what it's like to eat it from their own experience.

I bring a stack of cups to the chopping block, and Aparna pours a round of milk.

"I'll film since I already did it," Louise says, taking Duke's phone. "Calypso, are you going to try?"

Oh, right. I guess I have to. "Absolutely," I say. I survived it before. I will survive it again.

For a split second, I imagine Axel with us, laughing and trying it, too.

Aparna hands me a cup of milk, and I take a spot at the counter.

"Everybody grab their slice," Duke says. He's enjoying the spotlight, and I think he might be a good leader among the staff.

I pick up the slice of pickle, but since I've been handling cheese all morning, I'm wearing plastic gloves that prevent me from feeling any heat on my finger.

Duke holds up his hand. "Okay. On three. One. Two. THREE!"

Here goes nothing. I pop the piece of pickle in my mouth.

Even knowing what will happen, I'm not prepared me for the searing fire that flames over my tongue. Several people whoop and cough. Then we're all downing our milk, other than Duke.

He sniffs. "Some of you don't eat Thai and it shows."

This makes everyone laugh.

Louise passes him the phone. "Do we have an Instagram account for the deli, Calypso? This would be great for a post."

She's right. I haven't talked to Filo or Havannah about marketing. "Havannah might use it for the castle account. I'll check to see if we'll have our own."

Duke takes another bite of pickle. "We should. We're not the castle. And are we a Tasty franchise or a Pickle one?"

They're asking good questions. "I'll find out. For now, let's have Louise, Duke, and Aparna work the kitchen, and the rest of you be customers. Today, nobody order off the menu. Request unique combinations like you're a customer with random tastes."

"This'll be fun," Duke says. He adds the sliced ghost pepper pickle to its bin and walks it over to the sandwich line.

Soon they are humming along. This is good. They're doing well.

Now, if only I could get my personal life in this kind of order.

When the shift is over, I head to Havannah's office. Duke has forwarded me the video of the staff to show her.

I doubt she'll be there, but I pop in to check. Her assistant Monica waves me in. "Havannah is out in the barn. Apparently, an unexpected baby donkey was born last night in the storm."

"Is it okay?"

"Oh, sure. We have heat in there."

"Do you think it's okay if I go out there? I'd love to see the baby. I helped build the pens."

"Oh sure. We had a path shoveled out. Just dress for it. It's cold!"

I race to the employee wing to grab my new red coat and a hat and gloves. This is exciting, and way better than moping alone in my room.

I choose the exit closest to the barn. It's a good thing a path has been shoveled, because the snow banks are three feet high. I marvel at the glistening walls. Someone worked hard.

I follow it to the side door of the barn. The pens are empty of livestock, but the closest section is free of snow, and the wet dirt is sprinkled with white dust.

I open the side door and hurry to close it behind me.

The donkeys seem restless in the stalls. Poor guys. I wonder what the weather is like where they come from.

When I step out into the long channel that divides the two lines of stalls, I immediately see the makeshift pen set up for the mama donkey and her foal. It's cushioned with hay and has two heat lamps shining down on it. Jediah, the caretaker, sits on a chair nearby.

He spots me. "Calypso, our pen designer! Did you come to see the wee foal?"

"I did." I hurry forward. The mother is casually eating feed in a metal trough. The baby stands next to her, leaning against her belly.

"It's standing up!" I say, kneeling next to the mesh side of the pen.

"Oh, yes. Foals stand up for the first time an hour after birth. She's a wee bit wobbly, but looking good for a winter foal."

"Are winter foals more at risk?"

"Not really, other than we have to keep them warm. Miniatures take a full year to gestate, and we normally keep the jacks and jennies separate in the cold weather to avoid surprises. It's very rare for us to have a birth when it's cold. This jennie must have been determined to find her jack this time last year."

The foal's eyes keep closing for long periods, and it leans harder against the mother. Poor tired baby.

The barn is plenty warm, so I pull off my gloves and tuck them in my pocket. "I was looking for Havannah. Is she still here?"

"Aye. She's helping the others spread barn lime in the pens so we can let the herd out for some sunshine."

"Barn lime?"

"Crushed limestone. It dries out the muck and helps with the snow."

"I could do it, too."

"I'm sure they'd appreciate it."

I head toward the end of the barn, where snow flurries invade the open door. Vincent enters in a heavy black coat and gloves, pushing a plastic bin on wheels. "Hello, Calypso," he says. "Come to see the foal?"

"I did. Do you need help?"

"Why sure. You can take this spreader and fill it with barn lime. We're trying to stay ahead of the muck."

I take the handle. "Is it in the feed room?"

"Nah, the supply closet here at the end."

I nod. "Got it."

Vincent heads back out, and I roll the spreader to the storage room near the barn door.

But when I step inside, I drop the handle in surprise. It falls to the ground with a thunk.

Axel is here, pouring coarse white powder into another spreader, this one held by Havannah.

She looks at me, then her head whips back to Axel. "She's here," she says.

He glances up and spots me. "Oh."

I'm frozen in place. He looks perfectly scrumptious in a navy blue coat, black jeans, and a green knit hat that says, "Get Pickled" on the front. His cheeks are red from the chill and his eyes are bright blue.

"You're helping?" he asks. He turns to Havannah for confirmation and she shrugs.

"I was looking for Havannah," I say, "and I wanted to see the foal. I didn't know you were here."

"I asked him here last night for dinner," Havannah says. "We didn't realize the blizzard was coming. I had him stay."

I take a step back, torn between helping like I offered and running away.

"Now that you have Calypso's help, I'm going to return to my duties," Havannah says. "Thank you, Calypso. You're being very generous with your time. I'll text you when I'm available for a meeting. It's not urgent, is it?"

"No." I can't take my eyes off Axel. My boss has practically forced me to stay here with him by thanking me so profusely. "Just a marketing question."

"Perfect. I'll be delighted to talk to you about it later today or I can drop by the deli tomorrow. I trust it went well without Filo?"

"It was great." I'm watching Axel, who has resumed dumping barn lime into the other spreader. "We had a good team-building day."

"I can't wait to hear all about it. You two get this job finished. Thank you." And then she's gone.

The second spreader is filled with lime, but Axel doesn't look up. "If you want to bring that one over here, I can fill it."

I bend down for the handle and push it closer.

Axel lifts the bag, emptying it out into my spreader. "We should distribute these."

I grip my handle as he picks up his. Something in me is cracking, and I feel an overwhelming urge to tell him what I know. "I heard about your donations. That was a lot. Were those already planned, or…"

"No." His gaze meets mine, and everything in me flashes hot, like I injected ghost pepper pickle juice straight into my veins.

"Then, why?"

He breaks my gaze, bending down to smooth the top of the barn lime with his canvas glove. "I have no idea. I wanted the money gone."

"Because of what I said on the tower."

He won't look at me. "It's dumb. I can't even give it all away. Not easily. I talked to my accountant."

"You talked to your accountant about giving away your entire fortune from your app because of me?"

A muscle in his cheek flexes. "It doesn't matter. You feel how you feel. Probably I can't do anything about it."

I glance back at the open door to the storage room. Nobody seems near.

"Axel, I…it's hard to explain."

"I'm not asking you to explain it. I'm trying to accept it."

"I came from a very specific world."

"Debutantes. Cotillion. Country club."

I suck in a breath. "Yes."

"I saw pictures. After the day on the trail, I looked you up. You were different then. You weren't happy."

He saw that? My legs feel wobbly, like I'm that newborn foal. I sit on a hay bale. "No. I wasn't. My family had these expectations. I never got to be me."

"And you thought that because I had some things in common with them that I would be the same."

"Axel, I didn't know what to think. It was such a shock. I came here to be myself again. I knew that back in California I was following some sort of playbook I didn't understand. Then things got out of hand. I had to walk away."

"From your job. Your career."

So, he found out a lot. "Was it that easy to figure out?"

"You can't scrub everything." He shakes his head. "Actually, you can. If you hire the right company, you can get rid of your online history. But unless you take that very expensive step, there's stuff out there."

"Does anyone else know? I didn't disclose my degree."

He crosses the barn to sit on a hay bale near me. "Havannah knows. She's the one who originally told me. She discovered your background when checking references."

"Oh."

"She gets it. Don't worry. She said people come to the mountains to figure things out. So before I even knew you, I already knew this about you."

"And you didn't ask."

"I didn't care. I wanted to know the Calypso in front of me. Not some past version. The one right here. Who goes on a hike without knowing a damn thing about nature."

"And impales her tender bits on glochids."

"Who uses duct tape on a mountain trail like a *boss*."

Something loosens inside me. "So, now what, Axel Rose Armstrong?"

"You trust me, maybe?"

I pluck a piece of hay from the bale and curl it around a finger. "I can try that."

"We can take it easy. I'm in no hurry."

I might be. "Understood."

He stands up. "So how about we spread this barn lime, then I can make you a sandwich in your deli?"

I laugh. "I've been eating in that deli for two days."

"Oh, but I'm a Pickle. I know all the tricks to make something new and exciting from the same old ingredients."

"Says the man who chopped his finger on onions and made bread dough that looked like curdled yogurt."

"Ouch," he says. "Oh, wait. That's what you were saying when you peed on a cactus."

I push against his shoulder. "Coming from the nature lover who can't see a blizzard coming and drives over to a castle."

He sits on my hay bale and suddenly he's close. "Says the woman who doesn't realize how irresistible she is in red."

Our gazes hold. "You orchestrated this coat purchase."

"I did. I couldn't stand for you to wear anything else." His face is inches from mine.

"Are you saying I should wear red all the time?" My body heats again, and this time pickles have nothing to do with it. Except, maybe, this one.

"I'm saying you should wear it, unless you're not wearing anything at all."

I want to remind him that he *just said* he's not in a hurry, but then his mouth is on mine, and I forget we had this fight. That I was so worried. That we both made mistakes.

Because this moment is so incredibly right, so warm, so perfect, so in sync, that I can't remember why I felt I should be anywhere else.

31

AXEL

After Calypso and I spread the barn lime, we practically run through the tunnel of snow back to the castle. I'm grateful for crappy meteorologists, for Vincent's smart forecasting knees, and that I got stuck here.

We burst into the silent deli and flip on the lights. Calypso carefully locks the door.

I lean against the counter. "Why, milady, I think you have me trapped here."

She wraps her arms around my neck. "I think you promised me unspeakable acts in the pantry."

Given that Havannah practically shoved us together in the barn, I have a feeling she would not be opposed to whatever we do in her deli.

"I promised you food."

"Later."

I lift her onto the chopping block, spreading her knees so I can stand close. She's slightly above me, so I have to pull her head down to mine for the kiss of her life.

I want it to say all the things I thought and felt in the days we were apart. That she's worth losing my fortune, if that's what it takes. That I would never put her on display or make her be someone she isn't. That I like her exactly as she has been since she got here.

I think she knows it. Our mouths work together, not in a frenzy like I thought they might, but in understanding, in tenderness. I pull off her hat and unzip her coat.

"You have too much on," she says, breaking the kiss with a laugh.

I yank off my hat and coat and let them fall to the floor. "Done."

"Still too much."

I hold both of her cheeks in my hand. "Maybe we don't want to do this here."

Her expression is solemn. "Maybe not."

"I have the key to the secret suite."

Her eyes light up. "Havannah put you in there?"

"I insisted on it."

Her eyes mist over. "Because of me?"

"I'm pretty sure everything I've done in the last few weeks has been because of you."

She wraps her hands around my neck. "We haven't even been on a date yet."

"Dates are overrated."

"So, to the suite?" Her eyelashes are long and curled, and I want to memorize every part of her face.

"Just one problem."

"What's that?"

I let out a long sigh. "When I came over here, I was determined to make sure we didn't run into each other. To not break my word about giving you space."

"And?"

"I didn't bring condoms."

Her laugh is the best sound in the world. "I guess you can't get away with buying them in the gift shop. The whole castle would know within the hour."

I press my mouth to her ear. "I am happy to be of service to you again."

"I bet you are. But I don't feel at risk with you. Do you feel at risk with me?"

"I'm happy to knock you up and start a family."

She smacks my shoulder. "After two weeks!"

"Two weeks is a record for me lately."

This sobers her. "Really?"

"It's hard to know who's genuine and who wants the fringe benefits of money without caring about who is doling them out."

She presses her forehead to mine. "I get that."

"So, shall we make a baby?"

She laughs again. "I'm on birth control, you silly thing."

"Whew. Okay. I mean, I'm all in. But maybe waiting a few more weeks is best."

She laughs again, her cheeks pinking up. "Axel!"

"Should we name her Rose?"

"Why not him?"

"Done."

We both have a long, deep chuckle, then I slide her

forward and set her on the ground. "To the secret suite?"

She glances down at my jeans. "You might want to hide that before we go through the lobby."

She's right. I scoop up our coats. "I'll carry these."

She grabs the hats. "I've got these."

And then we're out of the deli, and taking the stairs up the tower to the Cinderella floor.

Then down into the clouds.

"I can't believe she let you stay here," Calypso says. "Yonder says it's almost never in use."

"She was mad I knew about it," I confess. "But don't worry. I didn't tell her you showed me."

Calypso drops our hats on the sofa. "I'm sure she figured it out."

"Not necessarily. We Pickles are scoundrels and would completely rat each other out about this. She's more likely to think of the cousins."

"She may not know I know."

Exactly. I fold the coats over the end of the sofa. "So, Calypso Invinia Ash, shall I ravish you in a forest, on a boat, or simply under the night sky?"

Before she can answer, I swoop her up and throw her over my shoulder.

"Looks like you're a pirate claiming your booty!" she cries.

"Yarrr!"

But I already know about more settings for the room. I played with them this morning, before I wandered outside and realized they needed help with the donkey pens.

I move to the control dial. Instead of rolling it, I push it in, then turn it. The light goes gray-blue, then trickles down the walls. The sound of a rainstorm arrives from the side with the windows.

"I love the sound of rain," Calypso says.

A smell permeates the room, fresh and clean.

I shift her in my arms and lay her gently on the bed. I got her back. She's not lost. It's like she said. She would adjust. She simply needed some time.

My body fits beside her like I was meant to be there. She lies on her back, and I trail a finger down the Tasty Pickle T-shirt that covers a black turtleneck. It doesn't matter what she wears. I want to remove it, piece by piece.

"I guess since I'm not wearing red now, I should be naked," she says.

"Exactly." I lean in to press a soft kiss on her mouth. We have all the time in the world. Outside is a blanket of snow. Inside, the perfect rain.

And here on the bed, we have nowhere to be.

My lips cover hers gently, taking in each corner, pausing on the fullness of the center. She parts, and our tongues get another reunion, warm and honeyed. I smile against her. "You had a ghost pepper pickle today."

Her eyes open. "That was hours ago!"

"It stays with you a while."

"The entire staff tried them."

"That should've been fun."

"I wished you were there."

I prop up on one elbow. "Did you?"

"I did."

"I'll be there tomorrow."

"Havannah will kick you out of this suite."

"Then I'll get another one."

I capture her mouth again, this time traveling down her jaw. I can't make any headway with the turtleneck, so I finger the bottom of both shirts and start pushing them up.

Her belly is warm and quivers beneath my hands. I feel no urge to rush. I measure the span of her ribs with my hand, bumping along every rib.

My thumb finds the bottom edge of her bra and slips beneath it.

She sucks in a breath, and I hold still a moment, letting her anticipate when I will touch her. Her chest rises and falls, waiting, then in one movement, I slide beneath the lace and cup her fully.

She sucks in a breath, her fingers reaching for my head. "Axel."

"Calypso." I shift to rise over her, using my hands to pull both shirts out of my way. They hit the floor, and I focus on the scraps of white covering her. This is in the way too.

I kiss the base of her ribs, making my way up. When I reach the bra, I shove it aside, swiftly taking a nipple in my mouth.

Her back arches and I slip my hands behind her, releasing the hook. Then the bra meets the same fate as the shirts and she is bared to me.

I linger everywhere, the round fullness at the base of her breasts, the space between them, then each puckered nipple in turn.

Her breathing is ragged, her hands gripping my hair.

It takes control not to rip the rest of her clothes off and sink into her. As her need rises, so does mine.

I unbutton the snap of her jeans and ease the zipper down. I remember this space well, and I want to be there again, but this time with my mouth.

Her shoes keep me from pulling off the pants, so I move down to unlace her sneakers. Then they are gone, and her socks, and I maneuver the jeans down her legs.

I kiss each part of her as it is revealed. Hip bone. Thigh. Knee. Ankle. I work my way down one leg and back up the other. When I reach the white lace panties, I press my face to them. I'm going to lick her until she screams.

I can feel her heartbeat between her legs. She's had to let go of my hair while I undressed her, and now she grips the pillow. I look up her body, the plane of her belly, the naked breasts, her chin thrust into the air.

The rain comes down, an occasional light peal of thunder breaking across the room. I run my thumb down the center of her panties, marveling at the warm dampness there.

Then I pull them down.

They slide slowly down her legs until I send them flying. Now I'm hungry, less able to slow down. I spread her thighs and press both thumbs to her body.

Her long moan makes my blood quicken. I want to feel her skin against mine, so I quickly toss the sweater and kick off my shoes and jeans.

When I fall between her legs, the soft skin of her

thighs presses into my shoulders, and her bare feet rest against my back.

I start with one long, unrelenting lick from top to bottom. Her whole body shudders, back arched, those beautiful nipples aimed for the sky.

I spread her folds and go in, my tongue learning every recess of her body, listening to her, feeling my way. I find that bud that drove her mad on the tower and draw it into my mouth.

She whimpers, her muscles quivering, thighs pressed around my head.

I love this, making her fall apart, this intimate closeness. I know her from the inside out, starting here.

I suck hard on the nub and suddenly everything in her tightens. I spread my hand across her belly, admiring how it tenses up, preparing her.

Then, with a loud cry, she lets loose. Her body pulses against my tongue, living and breathing as if this part of her has a life of its own.

I hold on to her, waiting out the orgasm, until she releases the pillow and sinks back into the bed. "Axel," she breathes.

"I'm here."

"I think I knew that."

I chuckle against her skin, pressing more kisses as I work my way back to her belly and breasts.

She reaches for me. "I've wanted to hold this in my hand since the moment I saw it."

"Mmm. Really?"

"Never get aroused when you have cactus spines in your parts. The blood flow is distinctly uncomfortable."

I smile against her neck. "I aroused you?"

"You have always aroused me."

Her hand slips up and down my cock, and I drop my forehead to her shoulder, reveling in every stroke. I have her back. She's mine again.

And we're here, doing this.

I will never allow anything to come between us again.

She pulls me forward to slip over her. "I'm trying to decide which way I want you."

"I'm yours at any angle."

"Mmmm."

Then, unexpectedly, she grasps my back, and we roll on the bed.

She stops on top of me, her knees on either side of my thighs.

"It's my turn to torture you into oblivion."

I'm more than happy to fall into the abyss.

32

CALYPSO

I haven't forgotten my new philosophy: live in the now.

I look down at this gorgeous, no-tan-line man, and I'm ready to sink him into me.

But I'm going to make us both wait a bit longer.

I shift above him, holding his length in my hand, and ease only the barest inch inside me.

He groans, his head thrown back, his hands on my hips.

He could shove me down with those powerful hands. If I had rope, I would tie down his arms. But that is a treat for another day. For now, he's letting me have control.

I can't get pregnant, but for a moment, I sit with the idea of it. His seed, flowing through me, creating another life that belongs to the two of us.

And for the first time in my life, I can see this future. I want it.

Before, I only saw the parent-child relationship from

my perspective as the child. Me, controlled by the people who brought me into the world.

But I can see something else. Looking at a child. My child. And giving it all the room to grow I wish I'd had.

What has this man done to me?

I slide him along my body, slippery and wet. He closes his eyes, hands loosely holding me.

It's nice, this anticipation, the last moment before we come together and see how our bodies respond. Another space will be filled, knowledge gained.

I want it so much.

I run a hand down his beautiful chest, dipping a finger into his belly button, then down his light fuzz of hair. The other still grips him, moving him back and forth. I'm ready, but this wait is so excruciating, so intense, I want to draw it out.

He lets out a soft growl, like a warning, and I smile. I'm getting to him.

I doubt I have much longer to tease him before he will take matters into his own hands. So, after one more slow, agonizing glide outside of my body, I let him slip inside.

His hands instantly grip my hips. My whole body shivers as if something has taken it completely over.

So this is what they mean by being possessed. He possesses me, and not just one part of me. All of me.

Pleasure sparkles through me like I'm made of magic. The fine hairs on my arms stand on end. Every nerve ending prickles, from beneath my scalp to the bottoms of my feet.

I feel him everywhere.

I almost forget what to do. I've done this act before. I know the motions. But the anticipation, the back-and-forth, the push-and-pull, and now, this perfect place with the thunder and the blue light and the fresh scent of rain — it's a complete overwhelm of every one of my senses.

When I falter over him, forgetting to move, he shifts my body himself. Then we work together, my distance, his speed. And the harmony of the two of us resonates like a tuning fork striking metal.

I never want this to end. I want to hold on to this high. But the tension rises in a slow build. My muscles tighten. He twitches inside me even as the strokes stay slow and languid.

Then I'm pushing down harder against him. And he's moving faster.

Neither of us feels in control as this act takes us over. The thunder seems louder, and the rain falls harder.

I press my hands against his hard chest, losing my way, not sure if I'm sitting or lying, if I'm moving or still. The world goes blurry and indistinguishable as every part of me ignites in the blossom of this orgasm unfurling between us.

I can almost see the fire licking through me, bright and crackling. I'm silent, then crying out, then letting out a long, keening version of his name.

He holds onto me, thrusting into the waves crashing over me. I feel the pulse, the rush of warmth.

We hold still, letting it all wind down on its own accord. The rain sounds fall to a patter. Axel draws me to his chest and strokes my hair.

I lie with my cheek to his shoulder, my eyes wide open. What is different this time? Why is Axel so unlike anyone else? What am I feeling?

My belly shudders, and Axel squeezes me more tightly. "You okay?"

I nod against his skin. My voice won't work.

All the things I've pushed against seem small. My parents and their petty criticism and their efforts to control me. Why had I fallen for that? Maybe at thirteen, it made sense. But when I graduated from college? Why had I taken that blind date with Jeremy? Why had I kept it going when we clearly had no chemistry, no attraction?

Was Jeremy plodding along, too? Or was he part of the problem?

How did I get to a marriage proposal with someone without ever knowing what this moment with Axel felt like? Is this rare? Or had I never given myself a chance, never trusted my own feelings?

I had almost walked away out of fear, but Axel hadn't let me.

I kiss his collarbone. This feels completely right. I have no hesitation, no resistance. Moving forward with Axel is like taking a water slide into a clear blue pool. Easy. Exhilarating.

I think my voice will work, so I try. "I don't guess Havannah will let us live here forever, will she?"

He presses his lips to my hair. "I propose you use your employee key to break into the system, erase all evidence of this room, re-key the fake maintenance closet lock so that only you can use it, and we'll live happily ever after right in here."

The system in the room must be voice activated, because as soon as Axel says "happily ever after," the entire lighting scheme changes. The lights slowly brighten, the rain sounds stop, and a pastel rainbow grows from the wall near the door, across the ceiling, and behind our heads.

"Oh, my gosh." I sit up to look at it. "It's beautiful."

Axel shifts into position beside me and draws me to his chest. "Havannah sure believes in her fairy tales, doesn't she?"

"Why wouldn't she? She married Donovan and got to build a castle."

"And her secret suite is her tribute to that fundamental truth."

I rest my head on his chest. "In a jaded world, this is her sanctuary within a sanctuary."

"And we have to leave it for others to share, too." Axel wraps his arms around my belly as we both stare in wonder at the colored light sparkling across the ceiling from some unseen projector.

"Not yet." I turn to face him, reveling in the feel of our bodies flush against each other.

He takes me in, hands on my thighs, and then there it is. One particular part of him is ready for more.

"How do you do that again so soon?"

He lifts me up to settle me on him one more time. "When in a fairy tale, be the fairy tale."

I gasp as he presses me down to fill me up again. "Axel Rose, I have a feeling this is going to be a very long night."

He fills his hands with my breasts. "It better be."

33

AXEL

The next morning is a crazy rush. Calypso has to dash to her own room to shower and dress for a day of work at the deli. I decide to see if it's safe to make a quick trip home.

The snow has let up, and the highway is plowed, so I carefully make the quick drive to avoid wearing the same clothes three days in a row.

I realize my mistake when I arrive at my driveway but can't get anywhere near my house. It takes some negotiating, but after offering to pay five times the usual fee, a company comes out to clear my driveway within the hour.

I'm impatient to get back to Calypso. To avoid a repeat of the snowed-in problem, or worse, getting stuck *away* from her, I pack a duffel bag of clothes to leave in my car. With things finally going right again, I'm not going to let her out of my sight if I can help it.

When I finally make it back to the castle and enter

the deli space, the staff is doing a conga line around the tables in the dining room.

Calypso is smack in the middle of it, laughing and kicking her legs with the rest of them.

She glows.

I like to think I had a hand in that.

When the staff sees me, they wave me over. "Axel! Join in!"

I guess when in a Pickle deli, you do as the employees do.

I insert myself behind Calypso just to have the excuse to put my hands on her waist. We snake around the room, back to the kitchen, and circle the chopping block before the song ends.

Duke, who is leading the line, immediately starts the song over. We're about halfway through this round when Louise stops abruptly, causing the rest of the line to accordion into each other.

"What gives?" Duke calls out, but then we all see.

Havannah has entered the deli.

Everyone lets go of the line and turns to face her. Duke fumbles with his phone to stop the music.

"No, no!" Havannah calls. "Don't stop on my account!"

She hurries to the end of the line and puts her hands on Aparna's waist, and off we go again.

This time when the song ends, Duke shuts it off.

Calypso looks sheepish as she approaches her boss. "Havannah! You came!"

"I love this," she says. "I've never seen any of my other crews dancing."

Duke pumps his fist in the air. "That's because we are the best crew." He dashes to the middle of the room and holds out his arm.

The other members of the crew hurry forward to slap their hands on top of his. Calypso passes Havannah with a smile and smacks her hand down on top. She says, "One, two, three."

The group says in unison, "Tasty Pickles taste great!"

Havannah claps her hands. "Definitely, no other crew has a cheer. What an amazing team you've built here, Calypso. How did you do it?"

Duke steps forward, his dark fingers spread on his green deli shirt. "It all started with my idea to eat the ghost pepper pickle."

Havannah laughs. "I think I've seen this story play out before. This is great. Calypso tells me you guys are interested in your own social media account."

"Hell yeah," Duke says, then claps a palm over his mouth. "Sorry for the hell."

Havannah holds up a hand. "Just don't say hell to customers. That's all I ask."

"We have developed an identity that might be unique from the branding of the castle," Calypso says. "The entire team seems to have an interest in creating an experience here that isn't all princesses and carriage rides."

Louise links her elbow through Aparna's, and they dance in a tight circle. "We have our own vibe."

"A vibe," Havannah says with a laugh. "You guys are making me feel old. But I absolutely agree." She walks to the dining room, brushing her fingers over the occasional table. "I was incredibly proud when we opened Tasty Mango. It was the first independent franchise of my grandparents' original deli. My parents had taken it over, but I was the one who argued that the *vibe* of the original was wrong for new and younger customers."

She holds out her arms to gesture to the space. "You guys are doing it again. Not with paint, menu items, or branding." She winks at Calypso. "But with your energy and your enthusiasm. I wouldn't be a very good boss if I didn't recognize that I had something special here. and let you all take the reins."

A cheer breaks out over the staff.

I have to hand it to Calypso. She's really done something here. I've never seen Havannah talk this way. I've been in all of my cousins' delis, including the original with Grammy Alma in Brooklyn, and none of them have an energy like this.

Havannah pulls out her phone. "Let me take a picture of you all to kick off your very own Instagram account."

"Don't forget TikTok!" calls Duke.

Havannah nods. "Whatever you guys want. We'll have you send whatever video and images you want to Paula. who runs the castle social media. She'll pass them through legal if she feels like she needs to, as we still have to worry about copyright infringement and song licensing."

A groan fills the room.

"I know, I know. I don't want to kill the vibe. But we will prioritize pushing you guys through so that you can capitalize on whatever crazy notions you get in your heads."

"Can we have random conga lines in the dining hall even when the customers are here?" Duke asks.

"I think that would be fantastic," Havannah says. "You have my official blessing."

"We're gonna pickle conga!" Duke says. He fires up the song again, and a cheer erupts. The regular crew reassembles its line, but Calypso walks over to Havannah. I follow her lead.

Havannah crosses her arms, looking us up and down. "You two seem both exhausted and happy. Is that good news?"

Calypso steals a glance at me. "Yeah."

Havannah elbows my ribs. "Good. Are you out of the suite?"

I nod. "I had my drive shoveled, and I stopped by home today."

Havannah tugs on her lanyard, which holds her hotel key card. "I kept Calypso's maintenance clearance on her employee key card. She has access to any empty rooms if necessary. Just make sure housekeeping knows you were there."

Calypso's cheeks pink up.

Havannah laughs. "It's okay. Donovan and I had a great time breaking in every suite. Axel's one of the good ones. I'm pleased for you both." She looks around. "I'm guessing Filo hasn't been here much."

"The storm has kept him away," Calypso says. "He's on some dirt road that's low priority for the plows."

Havannah nods knowingly. "And when he couldn't

be here, you made this magic happen. Interesting. I need to leave him on as manager because he has the experience for all the administrative and payroll tasks you aren't going to be familiar with for a while. But I'll be watching."

Calypso's face is a mixture of relief and concern. I wonder if she's thinking about her old job as an engineer and how this sideline in food service was never part of the plan. I reach out and squeeze her hand.

"Nothing unsanitary on the deli counter," Havannah says.

"We'll bleach it down," I say.

Calypso shakes her head. "You Pickle people and your weird ideas."

Havannah grins. "Do you think the crew is ready for a soft launch? No announcement. No grand opening yet. Just start taking orders. This is our slow season, so I wouldn't expect you to get overwhelmed."

Calypso straightens her hat, which got askew during the conga line. The dance is going strong in the other room. "I think so. We've been preparing all the menu items plus creating random customized sandwiches to make sure everyone is on board with whatever might get ordered. Three cashiers are trained, and I will slowly get everyone at least a basic knowledge of how to check someone out in case we are ever short-staffed."

"All very smart. I like everything I see. I'll get the graphics department to put together a menu board and a flyer for the rooms." She rubs her hands together and heads for the door. "Let's go for Saturday as day one. This is going to be brilliant."

When she's gone, I pick Calypso up by the waist to twirl around. "You are amazing."

But as I set her down, her smile doesn't quite reach her eyes. It's clear that the Tasty Pickle crew loves Calypso, and they are doing great work under her guidance.

But she's not quite convinced that this is the right place for her.

34

CALYPSO

The week leading up to the soft launch is easily one of the happiest periods of my life.

The snow melts away. Axel and I visit the newborn donkey foal, which has been named Blizzard.

The deli staff has a blast prepping menu items, practicing their duties, and coming up with wild ideas for the social media account. Filo leaves us with the daily tasks, only conferring with me an hour each day about ordering stock, payroll software, and how to monitor daily sales versus expenses.

All the skills are new and fill me with a sense of accomplishment.

Every night, Axel and I find a new suite to test out. We've broken in the vampire suite with its rich red velvet motif. The spring meadow suite was like being outdoors, with the bonus of a beautiful sunken tub in the bathroom, surrounded with live plants to feel like you are stepping into a pond.

Everyone wants to work on Saturday, so I schedule

hours for each staff member throughout the day. The early crew arrives at six a.m. to bake the bread. Axel gets up with me, and we head down to fire up the proofing ovens and prepare the ingredients.

Duke and Louise are already standing outside the door, eager to start.

"Star employees," I tell them and key us all inside.

When we flip on the lights to the dining hall, we all gasp with surprise.

The room is bright with green and white balloons with pickles on them. Streamers curl down each corner. New images are framed and hanging on the wall, all depicting our crew and our antics — the conga line, the ghost pickle tasting, the dough competition we held earlier this week, and a shot of all of us with our hands in the center, ready for our pickle cheer.

Tears prick my eyes. Havannah must have done this. It's incredibly special. I can't imagine the cold professional engineers at my old firm ever doing a conga line through the building. And I don't even know why not. Are they too serious? Is it beneath them to have fun?

Axel draws me close to him. "Look at this."

Louise turns to us, full-on crying. "This is so special." She wraps her arms around me, too. "This place is the best."

"I'm down for a group hug," Duke says, spreading his arms around our trio. "I'm seriously glad I saw this job posting a couple of months ago. It might be deli work, but it feels like it's our deli."

And that's exactly it. The Tasty Pickle doesn't feel like a place where we work. It's ours. We made it.

"We have to make bread!" Louise cries. "We don't know how many people are going to come in today!"

We definitely don't. Filo said to simply make our best guess. There are currently around one hundred occupied rooms, and twenty of them are on their second day, which means they may have already eaten in the dining room and will want a change.

We convene in the kitchen to mix the dough. We're starting out only with the basics, wheat, white, and sourdough. Soon, we're humming along, sifting flour and pounding the smooth mounds.

I glance into Axel's metal bowl. "Looks good," I tell him. "No more murdering yeast?"

He laughs. "I've set aside my killer ways."

We place the first round in the proofing ovens, then Aparna and Yvette arrive to chop. I step aside to give them room and check on the soda machine, the ice, and power up the register.

This will be fun.

Havannah comes down halfway through the shift. Everyone is buzzing with excitement. We've had about twenty customers during lunch and the entire staff has stayed on even when their hours are over.

She takes another picture with all of us under the decorations. "This is so great! Now someone make me a turkey and cheddar on sourdough!"

Duke races into the kitchen to prepare her sandwich.

"How is it going?" she asks me.

"Good. Everyone is having a great time, employees and customers alike."

She smiles. "I like that you say that first. Not sales or production. The people."

"I feel like the happier the employees are, the better sandwiches they'll make, and the better experience the customers will have."

"You are absolutely right."

I push in a couple of chairs. "Some customers were locals here for the weekend. They mentioned this deli is closer than the ones in Boulder proper and asked if we would do grab-and-go pre-mades and wrapped cookies."

"Cookies!" Havannah cries. "How could I forget cookies?"

"It's not on the menu sheet."

"I'll get with the restaurant. They can get us any ingredients we're missing in the short-term."

"Is there a specific recipe?"

"Absolutely there is. We can start the crew on them tomorrow. I'll get things arranged." She taps swiftly on her phone.

"And I was thinking, I know the stand in the lobby sells sandwiches. Would it be smart for us to make up anything that we can't keep — I'm thinking of the bread — into items for it to sell after we close at two?"

"Yes. Definitely. I always intended to switch out the products there with the deli's. Start sending them your overages, and we'll see how to transition." She looks up from her phone. "I'm glad you're here, Calypso. This opening has gone so much better than I could have hoped. Maybe, once this one is settled, you can bring your staff to the Tasty Mango or the Tasty Pepper and infuse those staffs with your magic."

Could I? I wasn't sure I was anything special. "I'm happy to do whatever you think will work."

Havannah tucks her phone in her dress pocket and accepts her sandwich from Duke. "Carry on, amazing people. I'll come back down near closing with the family. I'm really, really pleased."

Axel holds my hand as she leaves. "You've built something incredible here," he says. "I'm glad I get to be a part of it."

I squeeze his fingers. He's right. I'm happy. I have a place. I get to dance in a kitchen. I get to be with him in a different bed every night.

Even so, my stomach turns. This much happiness isn't something I'm used to. I can't trust it. If I've learned anything in my twenty-five years, it's that there is always a shoe that will drop somewhere.

Of course, I already know exactly what my downfall looks like.

And precisely one week later, it makes its presence known.

35

AXEL

I'm grateful I'm the one who answers the phone when the shit hits the fan.

"Tasty Pickle, where our tasty pickles taste great." I love saying it. It reminds me of the *Good Burger* slogan on the comedy show.

The rough female voice I hear next is icy enough to freeze lava. "Please connect me with Calypso Ash."

We don't get a lot of phone calls. And the ones we do get are generally from one of the rooms, asking if we can make a sandwich ahead for pickup, or if we have gluten-free bread.

Nobody's called for Calypso by name. Not once.

My neck prickles. I glance over at her. She's helping Louise figure out how to charge a man for a triple-meat foot-long.

"She's with a customer. Could I take a message?"

The line is silent. This makes my hackles rise. A salesperson who might call to sell Calypso their brand of coffee or their line of wax cups would be eager to give me their number.

"Tell her we're coming."

"Who's coming?"

"She'll know."

And I know exactly who it is. This is Calypso's controlling mother. I debate whether to play hardball, hang up, or laugh at her.

I go with, "That sounds ominous. Should we sharpen our axes?"

An indrawn breath tells me she didn't expect this response. "Who is this?"

Now it's time for hardball. "Someone who cares about her more than you."

And I hang up.

I stare at the phone, expecting it to light up again, but it doesn't.

Damn. They figured out where she is.

But how?

Duke starts the conga music, and the employees hustle to start the line. They do this whenever there's no one waiting to place an order and we're caught up.

Louise takes a picture to send to Paula for posting, and my heart sinks.

That's bound to be it. The social media account has Calypso's name on it.

I pull up my phone and Google Calypso Ash.

And there it is. Her picture. A video. Her name in multiple captions. She's listed on the castle site as staff.

Anyone monitoring the internet for her would find it.

I watch her dance in the line with the others, encouraging customers to join in. I compare this with the solemn, perfectly poised woman I saw in the pictures from before she arrived.

Her mother is coming. She told me to convey that message.

But she's not going to like what she sees.

I decide not to tell Calypso about the phone call until later that night. We decided a few days ago to stop dirtying up the bedding of random suites and we're safely curled together in her own bed. I haven't slept in my house in two weeks, but it doesn't even matter. I want to be wherever Calypso is.

She's warm and naked, and I fit my body against her back, drawing her against me. I slip a thigh between hers and fill both hands with her breasts. We've slept this way since the first night, and it's the most content I've ever felt.

I make sure we're well settled before I kiss her shoulder, hating to destroy our peace with this news. But I have to.

"Hey," I whisper near her ear.

"Hey."

I don't say more, not yet. I want to hold on to this feeling. Surely she's secure enough here, strong enough, to prevent her mother from rocking this wonderful boat.

"Axel?" She half turns to me, looking over her shoulder. "Is everything okay?"

I consider touching her, taking us back to the space we just left. Passion and murmurs, pleasure and release. It would be so easy. I know her body. I can take us there again.

But this has to be faced. "I got a call at the deli today."

She rolls over completely. "What kind of call?" The catch in her voice tells me she knows exactly what kind of call.

"She didn't say who she was. She asked for you and then said to tell you she was coming."

Calypso is so completely still that after a moment, fear rises, and I'm thinking the news has sent her into shock.

"You all right?"

Her body shivers. "My mother."

"I'm guessing so. Her voice sounded like the reason the earth has ice caps."

I don't expect her to laugh, and she doesn't, but a small amount of her tension goes soft. "So she's coming."

"I guess me confirming you were here was enough."

"You confirmed I was here?"

"I had no idea it was anything weird. She asked for you, and I said you were with a customer. Then she broke out the existential threat."

"I see."

"You don't have to talk to her. She can come here and ask for you, but nobody has to let her through."

"The deli is public. Anyone can come in the front

door and ask where it is." Her face is an unmoving mask.

Something's wrong. Way more wrong than I anticipated. Calypso won't make eye contact. Won't snap out of whatever's gotten to her.

"Is there something else?"

Her throat gurgles with the need to say something. She's afraid.

"Calypso. There isn't anything you could tell me that would scare me off."

"Jeremy."

"Who's that?"

"I was dating him before I left. He's the reason I left when I did."

A murderous rage rises in me. "Did he hurt you?"

"No. He… he asked me to marry him."

I suppress any outward sign of my surprise. I hold on to her body, keeping her close. "Did you get engaged?"

"No. I told him to give me time to decide and pretended it never happened. And later, after he left, I packed my bags, maxed out the cash I could get at an ATM, and took a bus to New Mexico. I didn't even take my phone. I got a new one."

"And your mother's phone call was the first thing you heard from them? They must have been frantic."

"I told my sister I left so they wouldn't call the police."

"Then why would they come? You can live your life any way you want. She can't force you back to California."

"I know."

"You have a life here."

"I know."

But her voice isn't convincing. "Calypso, you don't have to go anywhere. You can tell her to fuck right off and go home."

"She won't."

"We can call the cops on her."

"Havannah won't do that."

"You don't know that."

"I do. You don't call the cops on someone like my mother. I can't explain it. She has this way about her. She knows where to draw the line."

"I won't let her in."

"You won't be able to help it."

"Calypso! I'm not letting her manipulate you."

She presses her forehead to my shoulder. She's shaking.

I drag her close to me. I wish I hadn't told her. If I'd known that the threat of her mother would be enough to make her this unsure of herself, this doomed, I would have handled it myself.

But no matter what happens, whether Calypso fights or freezes when her mother arrives, I will absolutely not, no way, never allow her to crush Calypso's soul a second time.

36

CALYPSO

After Axel's news, every morning I get up with the resolution to text my parents and tell them to stay the hell out of Colorado.

But I don't. I don't want them to know my new phone number. I don't want to talk to them. I don't want to test my newfound freedom.

I try to never answer the phone in the deli. Axel becomes ever vigilant, either answering it himself or making sure anyone else who picks up the phone knows to fetch him instead of me.

But there are no other calls.

I try to recapture that happy feeling I've nurtured in the deli, but it feels so far away. And that doesn't make sense. Everything I enjoy is still right in front of me. Duke and his conga lines. Louise with her funny retorts. All the workers, happy and fun.

The work is light. We never feel pressured or overwhelmed. Anthony Pickle puts us on his list of breads with funny names, so there's always something new to laugh over and learn to create. Only yesterday we mixed up his new Monster Eye Pumpernickel with olives.

But a dark cloud has situated itself between me and the light. It doesn't matter that I'm twenty-five, that I have my own bank accounts, that there is no legal way anyone can make me do anything.

I feel the pressure all the same. The forces inside my head are strong, and their trenches run deep. I've only just begun to figure out who I am and the old me is trying to run me over with fear.

There is no glue in the cracks of my personality, broken repeatedly over the years as family obligations took over my life. I'm left with awkward pieces that don't fit together, pocked with holes and gaps. Unstable. Unsightly. And ready to shatter like a dropped lightbulb.

I don't like being dramatic. I don't like thinking that I'm weak and unable to stand on my own.

But I have no practice at it. I don't know what bold and confident look like. There's never been an argument with my mother that I've won. There's never been a directive my family has given me that I have not ultimately followed.

I tell Axel these things. He reminds me I got away. That the prison of the mind is as strong as one made of bars, but I freed myself anyway. All I need now is to stand firm when they come to test how hard I'm willing to fight for my freedom.

And he promises to be here when it happens.

And that's one thing I don't doubt.

The way we spend our days and nights together means it's possible that in the six weeks since our first hike, I've spent more hours with Axel than in three years with Jeremy.

This matters. If there is any glue, any one person helping fill in the cracks, it's him.

But despite the cloud, the worry, and the uncertainty that I can weather whatever might happen with my family, I do what needs to be done.

I show up for work. I bake bread with my crew. I pay invoices to suppliers and order stock. I sign paychecks.

I laugh sometimes, even if that bubbly feeling never takes over like it did before I knew they had found me.

The only time I truly forget about my complex situation is in Axel's arms. In those hours, my world becomes like that room in the secret suite. I can set the dial and sleep in the rain, on the bow of the ship, or deep in a forest. The real world disappears along with its troubles.

When my past arrives, it isn't who I expect.

It's the Saturday before Halloween, right in the middle of the lunch rush.

I'm helping Duke catch up on slicing tomatoes. Yvette is at the register. Aparna and Louise make sandwiches. Most of the seats in the dining room are taken. It's unusually busy, because Havannah is hosting a trick-or-treat event where families walk the haunted wing. The children collect candy from staff members at every door.

Our deli is much more affordable than the restaurant, so we're slammed. It's our first real test.

We're handling it. The staff members not on duty show up for conga lines and to help keep the tables clear. I am a strange combination of exhausted and exhilarated.

Then he comes.

When I see who has arrived, I gasp so loudly that Axel nearly drops the loaves of bread he's sliding into the oven.

My kitchen staff turns to me. I feel lightheaded, like I don't know which way is up or down.

It's not my mom. Not my dad. Not my sister.

It's Jeremy.

The door between the kitchen and the dining space is open because we've been passing through so often that it's been easier to keep it propped.

He stands for a moment near the entry from the hall, searching for me.

He looks exactly the same. Khaki pants, pressed shirt, boat shoes. His hair is the longest he lets it get. Probably he has an appointment with his stylist for next week.

He isn't bad-looking. But somehow the sum of his eyes, nose, and mouth don't work out quite right. I've puzzled on it, wondering what about his features don't add up to something anyone wants to swoon over.

But he's here. Our gazes clash.

Louise spots him and follows where he's looking. "Who's that?" she asks, too loudly.

Jeremy aims for the open door and has zero problems with strutting right through it.

Axel turns my way but hesitates when he sees a man

his age coming through the door. It's not what he expected, either.

He knows I don't have a brother, and this can't be my father. I'm not looking at him, but I sense the moment he puts the pieces together and understands that this is Jeremy, the man who proposed to me three months ago.

I'm glad I told him.

Nothing about Jeremy is casual, so he doesn't lean against the door frame or flash a sly grin. He stands near the chopping block with his feet shoulder-width apart, arms crossed over his chest.

Beside me, Duke stops cutting tomatoes.

The crew at the counter keeps trying to turn and watch, but they have customers.

Axel waits.

The noise from the families filters in. A man orders a tuna salad sandwich on wheat.

The silence continues, lengthy, painful.

It's Duke who speaks up first. "Calypso, this man isn't supposed to be back here. Should I toss him out on his—"

"No," I blurt. "I know him."

"I figured." Duke makes a point to aggressively resume slicing.

I realize I'm still holding my knife, and set it down. "Can I help you?"

Jeremy pierces me with his gaze. "You can tell me why my incredibly smart, well educated, and fruitfully employed civil engineer fiancée is cutting tomatoes like a common food service worker."

And that's it. The entire crew stops working to turn and look at him.

"That's not cool," Duke says, waving his knife in the air. "None of us said a single thing about your pasty-faced, Gap-wearing, stick-up-your–"

"Thank you, Duke," I say.

The girls whisper at the deli counter, and I realize Jeremy has said the word *fiancée*.

This is bad. My voice shakes when I call out, "Everyone, you've got this. I have some business to deal with."

"Let's go this way," I tell Jeremy, pointing toward the door to the hall.

Axel turns to us. "Should I come?"

I shake my head. "No. I have this."

"Are you sure?" The note of concern strikes me to the core.

"I trust that if I need you, you'll know."

I push the door open and exit to the hall. Jeremy is close behind.

"Who was that man? And why would he know if you need him?" His neck has gone red. That's rare. Jeremy doesn't get emotional about much.

I ignore his question. "What are you doing here?"

"I came to collect you. Margaret said she found you, and I should bring you home."

"I knew you were speaking to my mother."

"Why wouldn't I? The whole point of everything that's happened since we started dating was for her to be my mother-in-law. It's what we agreed upon."

"I didn't agree to anything."

He takes a slow, deep breath. I'd forgotten what that looked like, and how it felt to be treated as if I were a child who had to be dealt with. "We started slowly and built things up. I did the prescribed three years. Things between us happened at a proper pace."

"Are you talking about our relationship or marathon training?"

His disapproving gaze pins me. "When I acted on the understanding that I would propose after an acceptable amount of time, you pulled a disappearing act. Do you know how that made me look?"

I want to say, "Do you want to know how it made me feel?"

But it's already happening. My chest is going tight. I can't seem to find the words to argue with him. It's as though something is shutting down. Like now that it's hard, I can't find that willpower in me anymore.

Realization dawns. It's time for therapy. This is what it's for. Preparing for these moments. To have tools to deal with them.

I should have figured out a way, drawn money out, broken my lease. Something.

Because now I'm here, mute, weak, the opposite of what I want to be.

Jeremy takes my arm. "Calypso, let's go. I have two tickets back to California for tomorrow. Let's get a room in Denver and figure this out."

I want to shake him loose. I want to make him release me, so I can go back to my deli and my tomatoes and my conga lines and my Axel Rose Armstrong.

But I think I might throw up. Everything in my body

is failing me at once. My brain. My mouth. My words are gone.

Jeremy pulls me more tightly against him so it isn't as obvious that he's dragging me out of the castle. We cross the lobby and Filo's son watches us curiously.

The doorman opens an umbrella. "Can I assist you to your car? It's raining heavily."

Jeremy practically snarls at him. "I'm parked in the valet line. I didn't let them have my keys." A gray Mercedes sits in the circle under the overhang, blocking half of the entry. Jeremy didn't care that he caused an inconvenience. Only that he didn't get wet.

And he's only here because I made him look bad.

He opens the passenger door, not letting go of me until I'm safely seated inside.

When he walks around the front of the car, something in me snaps.

He's about to take me back! I have to run!

I reach for the door handle, but a car pulls up right next to us, squeezing in closely due to Jeremy's terrible parking job. The driver realizes he can't get out and looks behind him to back up.

By the time he's out of the way, Jeremy has started the car and shot forward.

The rain pours down on the windshield the moment we leave the overhang. Jeremy has to fiddle with the unfamiliar car to get the wipers going.

I spot the narrow side road to the trail we took for that first employee hike. There's a gate we will have to pass through if we go that way, and he'll have to stop. Then I can run.

"You're missing the exit," I tell him, pointing out the side road.

"Damn it." Jeremy swerves to make the turn.

We haven't driven far when he says, "This doesn't seem right."

"We're almost to the highway."

His mouth pulls down. "Are you going to explain to me what this was all about?"

"No."

He sighs. "Your parents will be at the airport when we land. They think it's best if you live at home until the wedding."

The wedding.

He's out of his mind. He thinks we can go right back to where we were.

"If there was any sort of dalliance with that man, I can let it go. Probably we should both have some sort of fling before settling down, anyway."

Now he wants a fling? Then for me to marry him?

My heart hammers. Nobody in this fucked-up family gives a damn about anybody's feelings.

I can't go back.

I can't.

We approach the gate. When we pull in front of it, he says, "Now what?"

And I know what to do. I'm not getting out in the rain. He is.

"Go open it," I tell him.

"In this downpour?"

"It's the only way unless you want to reverse all the way back to the hotel. There's no space to turn around."

He sighs again but puts the car in park and opens the door. The sound of the rain is a roar until he closes it again.

I wait as he walks up to the long silver bar and puzzles over the latch. Then he's figured out how to open it and walks it wide so the car will fit through.

I jump over the console, jam the car into drive, and gun the motor.

I don't even look at him as I pass through the gate.

I don't know where I'm going.

But I'm not going back.

37

AXEL

Calypso told me I would know when she needed me, and she's right. I stand over my cooling loaves for maybe three minutes when the urge to leave overwhelms me.

"Duke, you're in charge," I tell the young man, and I burst into the hall.

And they're not there.

Damn it. I knew I should have gone with her.

There are two places they might go. Her room or the lobby. The lobby is a bigger risk for him getting her away, so I take off in a sprint.

When I get there, it's full of families watching the rain fall. Nobody wants to go out in the downpour. Kids sit everywhere on the floor, sorting through the candy they collected.

I race to the doorman. "Did Calypso pass through here?"

He nods. "She got in a car with another young man."

No, no, no, no.

I dash out to the valet circle, packed with cars, more families trying to avoid getting drenched as they arrive for the trick-or-treat event.

I look in all the windows, but Calypso isn't behind any of them.

I run back inside to the doorman. "What were they driving?"

The man frowns beneath a tiny black mustache. "A gray Mercedes. I noticed because they blocked the circle for a time."

Sounds like something her family would do. "And they left?"

"Aye. Took off into the storm."

I walk through the crowd, pulling out my phone to text her.

> Where are you? Are you okay?

When I hit send, I demand that the universe give me an answer swiftly.

It doesn't.

I text again.

> I need to know you're safe.

Nothing.

I have to call. I punch her name and wait, my frustration rising with every ring.

Then it's her voice mail message, an automated version.

I want to smash my hands against the wall and roar in anger, but there are children everywhere.

"Axel! Axel!"

I turn at my name, even though I know it isn't Calypso.

It's Louise. She picks her way through the crowd, trying not to step on anyone.

"What is it?" I ask, praying against hope she's here to tell me Calypso is back in the deli.

But she passes me a phone. "Calypso forgot her phone, and she's getting messages."

I take it from her, my entire body flashing hot. Two missed messages.

Mine.

"Thank you, Louise."

"Is everything okay? Who was that man? Did he say Calypso is his fiancée?"

"He was never engaged to her. Keep the deli going, you and Duke, okay? You only have an hour to go."

"We will. Should we keep it open if we have a line?"

"Sure. And you can lock the door to prevent more from entering."

"Got it. I hope you get her phone to her." Louise looks at it uncertainly.

"I will. Thank you, Louise."

When she's gone, I stand at the glass windows, watching the valet try to manage the flow of cars. He has two bellboys helping. I should go assist. I'm not sure what else to do.

But then a bedraggled, drenched man walks up to

the circle. He's hunched over, arms bent as if to keep them off his soaked body.

When he gets under the overhang and out of the rain, he pushes his hair off his face.

It's him.

A snarl escapes as I lunge for the door. In three seconds, I have his wet collar in my hands. "Where the fuck is Calypso?"

He tries to shove me off him, but I hold fast.

"I don't fucking know, asswipe. She made me open some damn gate and then took off in my car."

I let go of him.

She escaped.

On a road with a gate.

I know exactly where she's gone.

I take off in a run back through the castle to my Land Rover.

.

38

CALYPSO

When I get to the end of the road, I'm not sure what to do. The rain is coming down in sheets.

I have an irrational fear that Jeremy will lurch up the road and find me.

Then what? Drag me by my hair to the airport?

Well, he almost did.

He got so far as getting me in his car.

I want therapy. I want it right now. I want to teleport a kind, soft-spoken woman into the passenger seat and have her get me started.

I need help. I need to be able to handle these triggers.

I want to be stronger than I am.

The rain shows no signs of letting up. I pat my pocket, but I already know my phone isn't there. I set it in a drawer when I was helping slice the tomatoes because it kept banging against the counter in my apron.

It's fine. I'll wait a few hours to make sure Jeremy has given up, then drive to the castle. I'll go in the back and this time I won't let Axel leave me. This never would have happened if I'd let him go with me.

I just hadn't wanted him to see my old life, the old me. I still don't.

I rest my head against the back of the seat. There's no telling how long I'll be stuck here.

Something buzzes near my elbow. I lift the top of the center console. It's Jeremy's phone.

Oh, he's going to be mad about this.

I pick it up. I can't unlock it, but there's a preview of the message on the screen.

> Do you have her?

My stomach heaves. It's my mother.
The next one arrives right after.

> We're getting on a plane. I knew you
> would botch this.

Then, one more.

> I'll file the mental health paperwork like
> we talked about. That will make her see
> reason. I'm sorry she's been more
> difficult than we figured. We tried to
> burn that rebelliousness out of her
> long ago.

What?
Oh, my god.
What was she doing? What "mental health" paperwork?

I swing the door open, not caring that I'm instantly soaked.

I smash the phone on the ground, then stomp it once, twice, three times.

I look up into the sky, the rain pounding my face, and scream, "MOTHER FUCKERS!"

I spot the trail ahead, and despite the wet and the cold, I start up it. Nobody is going to do anything to me. I'll hide on the mountain. They'll think I'm dead. Axel will find me. I'll be his forever secret.

I'm glad he's rich. We can go away. Live anywhere. A Swiss chalet. A castle on an isolated cliff. Anywhere they can't find me.

I stumble on the wet rock, but this makes me more determined. I watch my footing, trying to stay facing west. That's how I got from the castle property to Axel's trail last time.

I fall a few times, and end up with mud on my entire right side, but eventually I make it to the ruins of the cabin.

I jump in circles in jubilation. I did it! I found my way! No app! No compass! In the driving rain!

The storm slows down as I continue up the mountain. There's a fire tower with a bunker, and I know where the key is.

The hike is longer than I remember. The rain slows to a fine mist, but a teeth-chattering chill sets in. The light wanes. Were there flashlights in the bunker? I hope so.

I have to sit for a while on a log, my arms wrapped

around my stomach. I'm going to make it up there. I will.

I stand up and keep moving. I walk and walk, unsure how much time has passed. It's almost night.

It definitely wasn't this far last time.

I've taken a wrong turn.

I sit again, not sure what to do. The forest is quiet, other than the drips of rain falling from the leaves.

I have no way to build a fire. How cold will it get? Too cold to survive?

What have I done?

I need to *see*. If I could get a good vantage point, I could spot the fire tower. Or even Axel's house. He probably wouldn't care if I broke a window to get in.

I stand up and look around. The trees are mostly evergreens with Christmas tree branches that aren't conducive to climbing. Others are closer to scrubby bushes.

But there's an outcropping of rock ahead, clear of trees. If I climb that, maybe I'll be able to see something.

I clamber up the rocks. My nails all break, but I get to the top.

And I see it! The tower, the ladder, the concrete bunker!

I quickly make a trail in my mind, scanning for landmarks to make sure I know which way to go.

I slide down the rock and head back east. I went too far.

The first point arrives, a tree broken at the top and fallen over in a shower of dead brown branches.

I skirt past it and head for the next point, a group of trees with regular branches, like ones you might climb in a park.

I swear after today I am going to learn the name of every tree in Colorado.

Then, through the tree trunks, I see something gray. The bunker!

I push my hair out of my eyes, almost stumbling as I race for the base.

But when I get there, the door is already open! There's light inside!

And Axel is there, pulling me into his arms, wrapping me with a blanket.

His arm cradles my head. "You made it, you made it, you made it."

He's soaked, too, and his jeans are covered in mud. He looks exhausted. He's been searching for me.

We rock together for long moments. I weep against his shoulder. I feel like I've traveled for miles, for weeks, for years, to land right here.

When we finally pull apart, he's crying, too. I run my thumbs under his red-rimmed eyes. "I'm okay."

He pulls me in again. "I thought I was going to lose you."

"Of course not. You were in my head. I got to a high point. I looked for landmarks. I got here even though I went the wrong way at first."

"I never taught you any of that."

"But I knew it's what you would say. I heard you so clearly."

He lets out a choking laugh. "Then the two of us are closer than we thought."

A bolt of lightning lights up the room from the open door. "Let me call the search and rescue team," he says. "I already had them looking for you. The storm made it hard."

I nod as he steps outside the concrete walls to make the call. I glance around.

He has blankets, flashlights, food. I kick off my wet, muddy tennis shoes and peel off my soaked Tasty Pickle apron. Then I keep going. I'm wet all the way through. He comes in as I'm peeling off my panties.

"Good, get out of that wet stuff. Let me test the stove and see if it's safe. It might be clogged with a nest."

I wrap myself in the blanket and sit on the metal cot. Axel pulls on a metal handle and something metal squeals deep inside the pipe. Then he lights a few small pieces of kindling and rocks back on his heels to watch.

The smoke curls up into the stove. He nods and adds logs from a metal rack to the kindling. Soon, a roaring fire fills the space with light and heat.

I still feel completely wet, so I walk over to the stove and open the blanket, letting the heat dry my skin. Axel turns to me, his hair lit up by the flame.

"I wasn't sure I was going to get you back," he says. "And now you're here, like a goddess."

I understand how he feels. "Come here."

He knows what I mean. He peels out of his own clothes, spreading them in front of the stove.

Then we're both in the blanket, letting the fire warm us.

"What happened?" he asks.

"I froze. The fear took over. He got me in the car. Then I realized what it meant and made him turn down the wrong road."

"So smart. So very smart, Calypso. But why didn't you drive back?"

A sob steals my breath. "I saw their texts on his phone. They talked about filing mental health paperwork. Because I ran away? I'm an adult. They can't do that, can they? Even people with lawyers and money—they can't just declare someone a problem, right?"

He pulls me against him. "I won't let them. They might think they have money and power, but we've got Uncle Sherman and John Paul Boudreaux. Nobody messes with them."

He walks us over to the cot and sits us down. When we're cuddled in the blanket, our backs against the wall, he takes my face in his. "No one is going to take Calypso Ash from me."

When he kisses me, I know it's true. And as his mouth trails down my body, pausing on all the places he's learned so well, something settles in me. The panic dissolves to nothing. The fear falls away.

This is where I belong. In his arms. On this mountain.

And by the time he slips inside me, making me gasp, I'm no longer cold or tired. I'm sure. I love this man. I love my life here. I will slice tomatoes to be near him. I'll bake bread at six a.m.

And he will, too. He doesn't have to. He chooses to.

My body responds, and all the thoughts fly away as I focus in on this act, this perfect connection. I think I'll say it first, but then he does.

"I love you, Calypso."

Tears squeeze from my eyes. "I love you too, Axel Rose."

And this time, there's so much more than the pleasure, the collision of bodies, the desire. What floods me isn't just pheromones or chemistry.

It's joy. The sealing of our bond. Those fractured pieces of me, not held together with glue but forged with gold. I trust him with my life. And no matter what struggles I still have to overcome to assert myself and clean up the mess I left behind, I know I can do it.

Because together, Axel and I can do anything.

39

AXEL

I make sure Havannah throws Jeremy out of the hotel. I'm sure she did it more delicately than I would have. Someone drives him up to his rental car, and they follow him until he's off the property.

Calypso and I wait until morning to come down the mountain. Duke and Aparna open the deli without her, although she talks them through every step as we hike down in the shiny, bright post-rainfall morning.

It's almost noon by the time we're showered and ready to go down.

At first, her crew is careful not to ask questions. But when the deli closes midafternoon, Duke can't help himself any longer. "What in the Lifetime made-for-television movie just happened?"

Calypso catches my gaze, and I shrug. What she tells them is up to her.

"I had a stalker ex and a controlling family," she says. "That's why I came here."

"To hide?" Aparna asks.

"To hide," Calypso says. "And they found me and tried to make me go home. But I'm not."

Louise wraps her arms around her. "I'm glad."

We work quickly to finish the shut-down work, and I follow Calypso to her room. She has a big task left, and she knows she can't put it off.

We sit on her sofa and I hand her my phone so she doesn't have to reveal her number. She dials and grips my hand as she sets it to speakerphone on the cushion between us.

The voice I remember from the call a few weeks ago spits out a brusque, "I don't answer unfamiliar numbers, but I see this is from Colorado. Is that you, Calypso?"

She draws in a shaky breath. "Yes, Mother."

"What were you thinking, leaving your fiancé in the rain and smashing his phone?"

"He's not my fiancé, Mother."

"Of course he is! I helped him choose a proper ring. He said he gave it to you. We all think this little vacation of yours has gone on long enough."

"It's wasn't a vacation, and I never took the ring. I left him, and I left all of you, too."

"Don't be ridiculous. You have your apartment here. And your job. I contacted them by the way, and informed them that mental health was protected, and they weren't allowed to fire you without a discrimination lawsuit."

"You didn't need to do that. I arranged for the unpaid leave."

"You have been gone for months!"

"I'm staying gone."

"Whatever do you mean?"

She glances up at me. I nod and squeeze her hand. She's doing great.

"My move to Colorado is permanent. I have a job here. I like it."

"Calypso Invinia, you are not working in a deli. I forbid it. If my friends find out—"

"If they were actual friends, Mother, they wouldn't care what work your kid does. I only called to tell you to back off. Don't send Jeremy. Don't send my sister. Don't come yourself. I'm setting a boundary until I'm better."

"What do you mean, better?"

"Better at standing up for myself. I won't be home for the holidays. And you can stop talking to my old employer, to my leasing office, or anyone else you think you should meddle with. I'll fly out to handle it all when I'm ready."

"Good. We'll meet you with some professionals to help you see how far off the deep end you've gone."

"I'm getting my own professionals. It's time for me to say goodbye."

"Don't be ridiculous, Calypso. Helen's daughter also got cold feet before her marriage, and their psychiatrist got her right as rain."

"Goodbye, Mother." She punches the button to end the call.

I power down the phone. "In case she calls back."

Calypso falls back on the sofa and stares at the ceiling. She must be exhausted. It's been a lot. The hike, the night in the bunker, the emotional struggle.

I squeeze myself in next to her. "Let's lie here for a while. Let your thoughts drift."

"Is this what unemployed billionaires do all day?"

"I can't speak for billionaires. I'm getting perilously close to being only a third-billionaire."

This makes her laugh. "My head is buzzing. I love my job here, but it doesn't cover my rent in California, and I have six months left on my lease."

"I'll buy the complex then."

"Don't you mean loan me money to cover rent until I figure things out?"

"Nope. What's your address? Nevermind, I looked it up. I'll make an offer for it tomorrow. Then you can keep that apartment as long as you like."

"My mother has a key."

"Then I'll have it bulldozed at first opportunity."

The giggles take her over. "Because that makes more sense than re-keying my lock."

I snap my fingers. "Wait. Where does Jeremy work? I'll buy that company, too."

She smacks my nose lightly with her fist. "You can't use your money to solve every problem."

"Why not? Isn't it good for that?"

"Don't buy Jeremy's company."

"But I could be his boss. Then I could hire you and you could also be his boss."

She laughs. "No."

"Fine. Back to your old apartment. Is it nice? Well kept?"

"Of course. My mother wouldn't let me live anyplace shoddy."

"Then I'm buying it. Real estate is a brilliant investment. And I'll be your landlord." I roll on top of her. "And I will take my rent in sex."

"Axel! You can't say that out loud! You're horrible."

I nuzzle her neck. "And you're wonderful. Come on. Let's work on the new security deposit I added to your lease."

She wraps her arm around my neck. "I won't accept your buyout. But I will let you loan me your lawyer to help break the lease with the least penalty. Deal?"

I sigh. "Okay, fine."

"Besides, you've been living in my apartment for weeks. I think you owe *me* rent."

"Let me pay you in full right now." I slide her deli shirt off her shoulder and plant a kiss on her skin.

And we continue that way, with laughter and silly talk, until our mouths are too occupied for words.

There is a lot to figure out, but as long as we're working as a team, we'll get through it, one problem at a time.

40

——————

CALYPSO

S*ix months later.*

"Make sure the joists line up exactly right!" I call out as the crane lifts the renovated fire tower structure atop its newly fortified legs.

Four men in yellow hard hats, all in safety harnesses, stand on the circular platform to help lock the new tower in place.

This day has been months in coming. I headed up the restoration effort, trying to preserve as much of the original material as possible. I worked three days a week with a crew and historic preservation society to make sure we honored the original concept and design of the tower.

My phone buzzes. It's Duke from the deli. He's the assistant manager now that I'm only working there two days a week. But he's still pretty green.

I answer. "Everything okay?"

"Oven number one is acting up again. Do you have the name of a repair guy?"

"Radio Yonder and see if he can look at it. He's good with ovens. I'll contact the warranty company. The oven is not even a year old. It shouldn't be acting like this. We may have to send it back."

"Where would we make the bread? It's all integrated!"

"We'll come up with a plan. I'm sure we can use the main kitchen ovens if necessary."

"I hope Yonder can work his magic."

"Me, too."

"We'll see you tomorrow?"

"Yep."

I end the call.

Axel walks up behind me. "Exciting day. Is it all gonna line up?"

"Of course it will." I elbow him. "Are you saying I would make a mistake?"

"I wouldn't dare. You're the engineer."

We shade our eyes, staring into the sky as the tower lowers into position. It's a chilly April day, but clear and bright. The ground is dry. Perfect weather for the final stage of this restoration.

"Ho!" one of the men on the platform shouts.

Another responds with, "Heyo."

It's their own form of communication as they work to get the tower in place.

The structure slides to rest on the platform, and all four men rivet steel joints to reinforce the joists. Then a welder follows them, the bright streak sparking as he works.

"It's looking good," Axel says. "And then we'll need a new project!"

"The historical society gave me the locations of three more fire towers we could restore," I say. "If that's going to be our thing. Or we could find something else."

"I heard about an old metal bridge two counties over. It's no longer usable. We could tackle that."

"That sounds fun. You want to drive over tomorrow?"

"You work at the deli tomorrow."

"Right. Then Thursday."

He wraps his arms around me as one of the men climbs the side of the tower to unhook the cable tethering the structure to the crane. "Mmm. Deli day. I'm in the mood for unspeakable acts in the pantry."

"Again?"

He presses a kiss to my hair. "Mmm hmmm."

"One of these days, we're going to get caught."

"Nope."

The crane lifts away, leaving the tower behind. The men come to our side of the rail. "It's in."

I squeeze Axel's hand. "Shall we go up?"

"After you."

I start the climb up the bunker. We've mostly left the lower part of the structure alone, only adding a mattress to the cot, a generator, and a few other supplies. We've slept in there a time or two for a change of pace, especially once we no longer had six a.m. mornings at the deli.

I still have my apartment in the castle, but soon, I'll probably move into Axel's house. We spend most of our time there. It's a beautiful home. I hate that I disparaged it from the tower that first time I saw it.

We also spend a fair amount of time with his parents. I got to meet Rhett and Court when they came down for Christmas. They are a hilarious mess, and I see a different side of Axel when they're together.

I haven't seen my parents or my sister. Every time I think I'm getting better enough to risk a visit, one of them will send me an email or have some professional call the castle to talk to me.

This tells me they still resent their lack of control over my life. Mother threatened to disown me twice, and even father called once to ask why I was destroying my mother's life.

I hope that at some point we come to a place where we can have dinner without threats and disappointment.

But not yet.

Until then, Axel's mom is a great surrogate, and my deli family is all I need.

"Ready?" Axel asks. We're at the trapdoor below the platforms.

"Completely." I push it open and pull myself onto the wood planks. The workers pull on the metal legs of the tower, checking for any weaknesses.

I open the door.

Inside is the quarters for the fire watch. There's a wood frame bed, a desk built into the wall before the enormous windows, and a tiny wood stove. There is no running water, of course, and no bathroom. You're expected to go in the woods. We plan to add a generator for power and light.

I walk to the open window, not yet fitted with glass. That comes next week. The view of the mountains is glorious, the clouds encircling the highest peaks.

"You can see the castle from this one," Axel says, and I join him on his side.

Tucked into the hillside, the turrets of Havannah's fairy tale rise above the trees. Axel slips his arm around me. "When we drag our grandkids up here, we'll have to tell them that's where we met."

"But we didn't. We met on the trail."

"Do you plan to explain about your cactus needles and my swinging cock?"

"Good point."

I rest my head on his shoulder. Everything has come together. My work. Our purpose. Family and purpose.

I can't wait to see what we do next.

EPILOGUE: CALYPSO

Sweat pools on my lower back as we tromp up the trail. I pause for a moment. The air really is thinner up here.

"Axel, are you trying to kill me?"

He turns to me, grinning. "Not on your life.' He holds out his hand. "I know this is the toughest hike we've done yet, but it's about to be worth it."

We reach a rocky part and put on our gloves to climb them.

My hair has grown longer, and I'm glad for the ponytail. I need it out of my way for a workout like this.

Axel tops the rock and turns to help me up the last part.

"We made it."

I pull my gloves off, not wanting to sweat in them. It's late summer and while beautiful if you're lounging about, the temperature can make you overheat on a trail like this.

I tuck them into my backpack and turn around to see what Axel is talking about.

And when I see where we are, I can't catch my breath. "We're at the top?"

He nods. "Calypso Ash, you just scaled your first mountain peak."

The wind feels like it's blowing in every direction at once. I tuck a flyaway lock of hair behind my ear. There's no one anywhere. Only us, the blue sky, and an endless view.

"It's breathtaking." I turn in a circle. We're on top of everything. Sure, there are higher mountains in the distance. But from here, we are at the pinnacle. I breathe in. It smells different up here. Fresh. Clear.

When I look back at Axel, my whole body goes still.

He's on one knee, and he's holding a small red velvet box, open to show off a diamond that looks absolutely sinful.

"Axel?"

"Look at us," he says. "Up here. Together. This is as good as it gets. And I want to stay with you for the rest of my life. On a mountain peak. In a deli kitchen. And everywhere in between."

My cheeks are warm as I press my palms to them. "Axel." I move closer to him. His sun-streaked hair is wild in the breeze, and his blue eyes rival the sky.

"Calypso Invinia Ash, will you marry me?"

I nod and hold out my hand. He slips the ring on my finger, and I swear I gain two pounds.

We hold on to each other, the sun beaming down. No one can reach us here.

In fact, hey. No one can reach us here.

I stand on tiptoe to reach his ear. "On one condition."

He smiles against my cheek. "What's that?"

I step back and untuck my shirt and pull it over my head. "We hike the way down…" I unsnap my bra. "Naked."

"Now that's what I'm talking about." He drops his backpack, and in seconds, I see him the way I did almost a year ago. Bronzed. Fit. And one hell of a dangle. "I've been waiting for this moment my whole life."

We shove our clothes in our backpacks, and I tuck the ring into a zippered pocket deep inside mine.

Then we look at each other.

"No peeing on cactus," he tells me.

"No eating all the Laffy Taffy."

His eyebrows raise. "How did you know I packed Laffy Taffy?"

"Because you always do."

He turns his pack around and tugs out a pink package. "On one condition."

"What's that?"

"You kiss me first."

And we do, stark naked in our hiking boots, the wind in our hair—*all* of our hair—and the sun on our skin.

We're ready for the next stage of our adventure.

Thank you for reading *Tasty Pickle*!

I have a bonus wedding epilogue for this book!

Sign up for it at jjknight.com/getepilogue!

If you didn't read Havannah's hilarious first date with billionaire Donovan, where her water breaks and she tries to hide it, get yourself to Tasty Mango right away! Otherwise, see the entire Pickleverse of rom coms!

Characters You Met

You saw a lot of Anthony Pickle, who has the wildest fake-engagement-to-lovers romance in *Spicy Pickle*.

There were some crazy things going on with that princess Axel has to carry out of the ballroom in the Spooky Spectacular. Read that entire scene from two other points of view in the secret princess on the run book *Royal Escape*.

Havannah's billionaire husband Donovan looks like a champ with a kid compared to his brother! Read about **Dell's** hilarious disaster after Grace's secret mother leaves her baby on the billionaire's doorstep in *Single Dad on Top*.

WANT TO READ ALL THE PICKLEVERSE ROM COMS IN ORDER?

Visit thepickleiscoming.com for the complete reading order of the Pickleverse!

BOOKS BY JJ KNIGHT

Romantic Comedies

Single Dad on Top

Big Pickle

Hot Pickle

Spicy Pickle

Royal Pickle

Royal Rebel

Royal Escape

Tasty Mango

Tasty Pickle

The Wedding Confession

Second Chance Santa

The Accidental Harem

MMA Fighters

Uncaged Love

Fight for Her

Reckless Attraction

Get emails or texts from JJ about her new releases at www.
jjknight.com/news

ABOUT JJ KNIGHT

JJ Knight is one of the pen names of six-time *USA Today* bestselling author Deanna Roy. She lives in Austin, Texas, with her family.

To choose your next read from one of her fifty books, visit the web site **ReadLaughSwoon.com** to pick by book boyfriend, story line, heat level and more!

 facebook.com/jjknightauthor

twitter.com/deannaroy

instagram.com/deannaroyauthor

bookbub.com/profile/jj-knight

tiktok.com/@jjknight.author